A Fantasy Medley 2

A Fantasy Medley 2

EDITED BY YANNI KUZNIA

Subterranean Press 2012

First Edition

ISBN
978-1-59606-514-7

Subterranean Press
PO Box 190106
Burton, MI 48519

www.subterraneanpress.com

To Bill Schafer
and Josh Parker

TABLE OF CONTENTS

Quartered

TANYA HUFF

"Hang on, you fool!"

"I'm trying to!"

Evicka glanced up as the wind ripped the banner from the hands of the workman on the ladder. The painted canvass, flapping like a bird with a broken wing, was heavy enough to hurt any of the half dozen people crossing the courtyard even without considering the added weight of brass grommets and dangling lengths of knotted rope. She Sang the notes to call the kigh then Sang their ethereal bodies around the banner, still Singing as they pushed it over to the wall where it slid to the cobblestones disturbing nothing but a damp and disgruntled pigeon. She could feel people watching from the windows but that was hardly surprising. People always watched bards.

"My thanks, Evicka!"

"Happy to help." As the foreman made his thoughts on dropping banners clear, Evicka whistled a gratitude but waited until the kigh actually left before continuing toward the Bardic Hall. The death of King Theron followed by the coronation of his daughter Queen Onele had kept more kigh than usual around the Citadel as the bards of Shkoder had worked to keep as much of the country as possible informed. After a month of being constantly on call, of being sent from Elbasan, the capital, out to all six provinces and back again, the kigh—air, water and fire—had begun to believe their presence was required even when it most certainly was not. Only the earth kigh who ignored all but the most powerful bards during the cold of Fourth Quarter were behaving.

The new queen had put her foot down when the window in her private dining room had blown open and a cup of wine had landed in her lap.

"It was the first quiet moment I'd had to myself in over a month," she'd snapped at the Bardic Captain, all the bards present in the Citadel gathered in a loose semi-circle behind him. *"Fix this."*

Evicka had spent the morning up on the west battlements Singing gratitudes and dismissing as many of the kigh as could be convinced to go. She could faintly hear the Songs continuing but her last shift had ended at noon and the moment she got the final word from the Bardic Captain, she was Walking south. Although she enjoyed city life, she found herself looking forward to the solitude of the road.

Except for a fledgling racing toward the practice rooms, drum in one hand, pipes in the other, the Bardic Hall itself was pleasantly empty and Evicka took the stairs up to the captain's office two at a time. Outside his door, she unbuttoned the oil-skin jacket she'd needed on the battlements, checked the sweater under it for stains, and knocked.

"Come in, Evicka."

Older bards said that Liene, the old Bardic Captain, could tell a bard by their knock. She'd been a percussionist though so Evicka, who'd still been a fledgling when Liene retired, believed it. Evicka suspected Kovar, the new Bardic Captain, just expected his Bards to be on time for their appointments.

He looked up from a pile of paperwork when she came in and managed a weary smile under the arc of his waxed mustache. "I envy you the road."

Evicka spread her hands. "Come with me, Captain."

"If only I could." He couldn't, of course, which was why she'd made the offer. She didn't dislike the captain but Walking with him would be like traveling with a fussy maiden aunt. A fussy maiden aunt who Sang all four Quarters but still. He rubbed at his forehead with an ink stained hand and said, "You're Walking across Somes to the Giant's Gap, back to Vidor, and home, right?"

"That's right."

He gestured at a chair but she shook her head, too ready to Walk to sit still. Fortunately, the captain didn't care as long as she listened. "Pjazef is heading home with the Duc so the coast road and Somes itself is covered. You'll be visiting the small villages and holdings inland."

"That's right," Evicka said again and wandered over to peer at the large map of Shkoder on the wall facing the desk. Not only were the six provinces and their capitals marked, but every one of the aforementioned small villages and holdings. She was impressed by how tiny the scribes had managed to write. The bards, of course, didn't travel by map as much as by the kigh, going where needed as often as where expected.

"While you're out, I need you to cross to Bicaz. I know, a much longer Walk than planned," he added as she turned. "Let me explain." Palms flat on the desk, Kovar squared his shoulders and Evicka braced herself. This was the captain's *I'm about to say something important* posture. "I need you to check on the timber-holding the late king granted to Vireyda Magaly and Gyhard i'Stevana."

It took Evicka a moment to find it on the map. Just barely over the border, it wouldn't be far out of her way—the kigh had certainly taken bards further off their planned route. Frowning slightly, she turned again. "Is there a problem?" The holding wasn't far as the bard Walked from Ohrid and Ohrid had a Bardic Outpost. "Isn't Stasya keeping an eye on things."

"Stasya is…"

"Old?" Evicka offered as the pause lengthened. Stasya was in her forties, as old or maybe older than the Bardic Captain. And it *was* Fourth Quarter when only the younger bards dared the weather off the main roads.

Kovar snorted. "Biased. Stasya may be biased. Annice has a history with Vireyda Magaly, through her daughter and Annice is not…clear-sighted where her daughter is concerned. If Annice has biases, Stasya has biases. You can be objective where they cannot."

"I see." Bouncing up and down on her toes, Evicka realized the Bardic Captain was placing a great deal of trust in her.

Vireyda Magaly was an ex-Imperial Assassin who'd come to Shkoder with her lover, Gyhard i'Stevana, sharing her body. Actually sharing her body. She'd helped the bards identify the fifth kigh because it had been impossible for them not to acknowledge she had two. Two kigh. One body. Following close on her heels—their heels?—had been a crazy old man who'd killed and then stuffed the fifth kigh back into the dead, gathering a grotesque family. Vireyda and Gyhard and Vireyda's brother Albannon—also an ex-Imperial Assassin—and Annice and Annice's daughter Magda, and another bard named Karlene had worked together to stop him and, when it was all over, Gyhard had a body of his own.

Evicka had been on her first long Walk north when it happened so she'd met neither Vireyda or Gyhard. The Recalls of the bards involved suggested the songs had only barely been exaggerated for effect.

Kovar made no secret of mistrusting Gyhard. He considered him an abomination. Not because his kigh shared Vree's body, but why it had come to be there. Evicka supposed she understood the captain's point. If jumping from body to body one step ahead of death didn't take a person out of the Circle, she couldn't think of what would.

But according to Annice's Recall, he was no longer capable of it.

Which brought her around to the captain thinking she could be objective where Annice—the Princess Bard with a long and complicated story of her own as well as three really, *really* bad ballads written about her—and Stasya couldn't. His faith in her was an incredible compliment. She hadn't known the captain thought that highly of her. Or any more about her than he needed to for them both to do their jobs.

Bouncing back and forth, heel to toe, she considered how she felt.

A little surprised. Pleased. Flattered.

"What are you worried about?" When the captain frowned, she grinned. "You have to be worried about something, Captain, or we wouldn't be having this conversation."

The blue beads threaded onto the ends of his mustache trembled as he nodded. "Not something. Someone. Gyhard i'Stevana."

"Not the assassin?"

"She killed, he murdered. There's a difference. He is, in fact, a multiple murderer, pardoned against my advice, in control of an Imperial Assassin. A blade of Jirr. One of the Empire's most deadly weapons. Her brother Albannon, the only person who might have any chance of stopping her, is currently out of the country. I believe that if Gyhard is going to try something, these first few years of a new reign would be the time."

Evicka blinked, trying to absorb these new details. "He lives in a timber-holding in Bicaz. What do you think he's going to try?"

"I don't know." Kovar spread his hands. "But a man who can live several lifetimes by moving his kigh from body to body could try anything."

She couldn't argue with that.

"I need you to be my eyes and ears," Kovar continued. "No, more than that; the Bards of Shkoder weave the pattern that keeps the country safe. I need you to be the eyes and ears of Shkoder."

Cheeks flushed, Evicka nodded. "I can do that."

☙❧

"Might be snow tonight." Marija pulled down her scarf and blew her nose. The two guards on duty at the Citadel Gate with her backed a little further away. "But they're saying clear tomorrow."

Evicka winced at the rough edge to the other bard's voice. "Have you seen the Healers about that?"

"What's the point? Drink this and you'll be better in ten days. Don't drink it and you'll be better in ten days." Marija snorted and had to blow her nose again. "Enough hot water and honey and I can Sing and that's all that matters. You're Walking small holdings in Somes, right?"

"That's right."

"It's mid afternoon." Marija squinted at a silver gray sky. "You won't get far before dark."

"I'm spending the night by the south gate."

"Luvin at the *Bawdy Cricket*. Good." Further opinion got lost in a fit of coughing, but Evicka didn't need to hear it. Taking the memory of a warm and willing body out on a Long Walk bordered on bardic cliché.

"Sweet songs, Marija."

Only a bard could have heard *smooth roads* through the handkerchief.

☙❧

A week out from Elbasan—a week of Singing confidence to people who'd lived their whole lives under King Theron and were worried about changes under a new queen—and Evicka headed southwest off the Coast Road, into the interior of Somes and the first of the small villages. She picked a pair of skis out of a Bardic Closet in the last inn before she left the coast and was in snow enough to use them by the time she stopped for lunch. Skimming along the trail, her body slipped easily back into a motion learned in childhood. By the time she reached the village, her hat hung by its strings and sweat dribbled along her spine under the added insulation of her pack.

As she passed between the first houses, a pair of dogs raced toward her ignoring the boy charging after them, screaming at them to stop.

Evicka waited, leaning on her poles. When the first dog reached her, hackles up, head down between his shoulders, she used enough voice to put him on his belly in the snow. When the second reached her, he took his cue from the first.

"Oh my gosh, you're a bard!" The boy wheeled around without stopping. "I gotta tell my mom! Puddles! Thrasher! Come!"

Abandoned, she found what passed for a tavern on her own, a square room at the front of the brewer's house. Skis stacked on the rack outside, she pushed open the door. By the time the villagers began to gather, she was sitting by the fire with a rabbit pie and a mug of ale, her flute on the table, her small harp warming beside her.

Both harp and strings would have plenty of time to warm. She was the first bard they'd seen since Fourth Quarter festival when Jarwin had Sung the sun's return and they wanted news more than entertainment. When as many as were coming had gathered, she Recalled King Theron's death and the official mourning, allowing her flute to speak when grief tightened her throat. Many of her listeners were crying openly so she moved from grief to hope to joy, guiding them through their emotions until the entire room leapt to their feet and cheered at Queen Onele's coronation.

Evicka listened to the excited chatter as she began to string her harp. This was why she was on a Long Walk in Fourth Quarter. The Bardic Captain was right. The bards wove the pattern that kept Shkoder together. She'd never seen it so clearly before.

And if he was right about that…

In the holdings, she played in the common room where the extended family gathered for food and fellowship. Sometimes the holdings were small enough that the room was a kitchen with few delusions of grandeur and sometimes the holdings had spread a couple of generations around in cottages of their own and the room was the next thing to a village inn. She shortened or lengthened the Recall as needed, Sang the old favorites, taught new songs to those with musical if not bardic abilities and spent three days in a cattle-holding Singing the comfort of the Circle to the dying matriarch while they waited for the priest.

She often had company on the trails. Escorting a bard was reason enough for the young to strap on skis, risk the weather, and seek the company of those who weren't sisters, brothers, or cousins.

Evicka considered staying at the Giant's Cleft for First Quarter Festival, but the skies were clear, the weather holding, and she was pretty sure she could make it to Fox Hollow Mine in two days. Just after rising, she Sang a kigh off to the Bardic Captain with news of the pass, kissed both guards goodbye, and pushed off.

The freezing rain started just before dark. Although the road to the mine wasn't particularly steep, ice made the next day's travel fast enough that kigh wove around her head without being called.

Snow kept her at Fox Hollow Mine for the next six days. She Recalled the death of the king, the coronation of the queen, checked to be sure the new tunnel wasn't heading toward water, and played harp/quintara duets with the foreman.

"Where to next?" he asked when it was finally safe to move on.

"Harap i'Destori's timber-holding then another across in Bicaz."

"You're checking up on the ex-assassin?"

Evicka kept her gaze on her bindings. "Why do you ask?"

"The bards wrote songs about her. I figured they were interested."

Not so much in *her*. "We're suckers for a love song and Gyhard's..." She let her voice trail off.

"Changed by love, ain't he." When she straightened, he shrugged. "I only know what the song says. Me, I like the song about her brother, the one that's bodyguard to the prince." When Evicka frowned, confused by the sudden change of topic, he grinned. *"Assassin's Love Song.* You gotta know it. Well struck the writhing victim cries upon the weapon's kiss. Sweet pain I sheath your blade and die, for truth you did not miss." He waggled his eyebrows at her. "Now that's art."

"*You'd* think so." He smirked and she held out her fist, pole dangling from the strap around her wrist. "Thank you for your hospitality."

The new snow made the three nights sleeping rough almost comfortable but as she reached Harap i'Destori's timber-holding, it started to rain. It was rain/snow/rain the whole of her stay and the day she left, dark clouds crouched low on the horizon.

"Be careful." Toryin, Harap's eldest daughter, tucked Evicka's scarf securely into her collar. "Snow pack's unstable this time of year and if you head straight across, you'll be covering a lot of uneven ground. Why not go downriver to Allin's Mill, take the road into Bicaz, then up river from Janinton?"

"Because in a perfect world..." Evicka frowned at the horizon. "...that would take about ten days. I'm there in three as the kigh flies."

"The kigh fly," Toryin muttered. "Bards don't."

Was Toryin worried about the journey or the destination, Evicka wondered. "So..." She tried to sound like it didn't matter and had a horrible feeling she'd failed dismally. "...what can you tell me about them?"

"About who?"

"Gyhard i'Stevana and Vireyda Magaly. At the timber-holding."

"Never met them. But word is at the mill, by way of Allin's cousin's boy in Janinton, he knows what he's doing with wood. She lets him take the lead."

Exactly what Kovar had been afraid of.

"I heard a few folk headed out there. You know, ones at loose ends." Toryin made *loose ends* sound like *pulling the wings off flies.*

That was worse than Kovar had feared.

Out on the trail, Evicka called a kigh and sent this new information back to the Bardic Hall. The next day, a kigh brought instructions to be careful.

"Careful? Really? I figured I'd challenge an assassin, a crazy man, and their acolytes to a duel. Don't tell him that!" she added as the kigh flew lazy circles around her, looking intrigued. She Sang a gratitude and dismissed it before it got her in trouble.

Trail conditions went from bad to worse. The snow was wet, water dripped from both bare branches and evergreens, and when she stopped to rewax her skies the cold crept in under damp clothes. She couldn't remember the last time she'd had to put someone to sleep as a defensive move, mostly because she didn't think she ever had, so what was she supposed to do, exactly, if a man who'd taken himself outside the Circle, one of the legendary blades of Jiir, and their acolytes had to be stopped?

Evicka hadn't expected to be happy to see the timber-holding—not with the danger posed by the inhabitants—but by the time she crested a hill and looked down into the river valley, she was too thrilled by the prospect of dry boots to care if the fire was in or out of the Circle. A high wooden stockade surrounded the buildings and she could see two lines of smoke smudging the sky.

This was it. Eyes and ears of Shkoder.

Settling her pack on her shoulders, she dug in her poles, and pushed off.

Dark splotches marked churned up snow outside the closed gate. As she came closer, *dark* became *red* became *blood*...

Were the young men and women *at loose ends* used as targets by the assassin? She had to practice. Timber-holdings were dangerous places and "accidental" deaths not uncommon.

Weight on her poles, Evicka got her breathing under control and called a kigh, sending it over the stockade walls. If the kigh returned to describe bodies or weapons or unnatural acts, would she be shot down before she reached safety? Should she enter, pretend nothing was wrong and assume she could Sing them asleep before they killed her? Would she...

A deer?

Relief made her knees weak and she felt a little foolish. Even if Gyhard did have the assassin practicing her craft, he wouldn't have her do it right out where anyone could see. Of course, who'd wander by to witness it way out here...

"Are you coming in or passing by?"

Choking on spit would be an embarrassing way to die, Evicka admitted as she coughed and tried to catch her breath. She hadn't heard the small door to the right of the big gates open, hadn't seen the young woman standing there until she'd spoken.

This had to be Vireyda.

She looked small under the layers of sweaters and scarves and quite possibly the lumpiest hat Evicka had ever seen. She should have looked overwhelmed by so much bad knitting but she didn't. Evicka had no idea how someone could look competent just standing, holding a large bucket in one hand and a short handled shovel in the other, but she did.

Her skin—what could be seen between hats and scarves—was a deep olive. Her dark eyes, large and almond shaped. She was beautiful; the songs were right about that.

She set the bucket down beside the blood and began shoveling the stained snow into it.

"Vree!" A tall blond man stripped down to his shirt, splash of blood on one sleeve, charged out through the door. "I said, I'd get it."

"I heard you."

"You hear me but..." He stopped. Peered at Evicka from under a messy fringe of hair. Frowned. "Who are you?"

"She's a bard," Vree answered before Evicka could. "Skied over from Harap's."

Evicka tried to look at them both at once. "How...?"

"Shape of a harp case in your pack and your tracks come down the hill, not up the river."

Actually that was pretty obvious.

"And," Vree continued, "a breeze lifted his hair just before I came out. There's not enough wind today for that kind of an eddy inside the stockade."

"She notices things," the man said, as Evicka closed her mouth. He held out his fist. "Gyhard i'Stevana."

He didn't look like a man who'd removed himself from the Circle. He looked like a man. He looked tired. Frustrated. Like he was waiting for her to reply. "Evicka..."

He followed her gaze down to his fist. "The blood. Right. Sorry. Found a deer this morning in a crevasse with a broken leg. Put him out of his misery and figured there was no point in wasting the me...Vree!"

Eyes rolling, Vree allowed him to take the full bucket. "I'll take the bard inside then."

He glanced between them, expression suddenly unreadable. "You do that."

If she shuddered, Evicka figured it could be blamed on the cold.

The open area inside the stockade looked like a butcher's yard. An older man shoveled stained snow into a bucket while a young man and woman stretched the deer hide out on a frame. None of them looked like they'd ever pulled the wings off flies.

"I wanted to hang it…" Vree took Evicka's poles as the bard bent to undo her bindings. "…but Gyhard wanted it butchered immediately."

"And you always do what he wants?" Evicka kept her tone light, gossipy.

The ex-assassin stared at her for a long moment, then said, "No, not always."

But she would say that, wouldn't she?

Handing Evicka back her poles, Vree put two fingers in her mouth and whistled. Work stopped. "Merlyn." The older man studied her from under lowered brows. "Hanya and Pjason." The couple nodded in unison. "Donal." A large, muscular young man appeared around the corner of the stable, lowbow in one hand. "This is Evicka. She's a bard."

Evicka suddenly found herself surrounded by people helping her out of her pack, taking her skis away somewhere safe—somewhere she couldn't find them?—offering a hot bath, hustling her inside. She paused on the main building's long porch to answer one of Donal's questions and saw Vree and Gyhard by the gate.

Vree spoke briefly. Gyhard's reply went on about three times as long. It looked as though he'd asked her to do something. Vree refused. He asked again. The second refusal was short and to the point. Too many people were talking around her for Evicka to hear what was said but she had no trouble making it up.

The bard will find out.

I know. You'll have to kill her before she tells the kigh my…I mean, our plans.

I'm an ex-assassin.

There's no such thing. You can kill her tonight.

No.

That final no, at least, Evicka was positive about and she held tight to it as she followed Hanya into a small room off the kitchen. She felt herself relaxing in the heat until she realized she was standing in what looked like an Imperial bathing room.

"I know," Hanya laughed. "Vree insisted on it and Gyhard built it. Apparently, they bathe a lot in the empire. Who knew? Well, I expect you knew because you're a bard and bards know everything but it sure was a big surprise to me. Bathed more since Second Quarter than in the whole rest of my life." She smiled thoughtfully. "It's funny what you get used to. Gyhard had to insist Donal use it but it makes Vree happy so…"

"He's invested in keeping Vree happy is he?"

Hanya flushed, hands twisting in the bulk of her sweater. She looked as though she knew she'd said more than she should have. "He has his reasons."

Evicka thought of using Command, of forcing Hanya to tell her just what those reasons were, but she'd have to justify it later and she was so tired of being cold. She stripped off her damp clothes and took a step toward the deep inset bath.

Hanya touched her arm. "You get clean first, over the grate there. Draw what water you need from the boiler. There's fire underneath but it's designed so it don't go out."

"And Ghyard built this?"

She glanced over her shoulder at the door. "He's smart. Knows lots of stuff."

"You know his background…"

Her brows drew in. "Course I do. We all do. Can't help it what with the bards singing about him. We don't care." That phrase had the force of repetition behind it. "We have a place here." She closed her mouth with a snap as if afraid of what else she might say, turned on her heel, arms draped with damp clothes, and left Evicka alone.

Gyhard had brought imperial building techniques into the heart of Bicaz.

What else had he brought?

Besides an Imperial Assassin.

Evicka stayed in the hot water until her fingers puckered then reluctantly climbed out and wrapped herself in a bathsheet. Her pack wasn't in the bathing room and she could only hope they'd hung *all* her clothes before a roaring fire. Fingers about to close around the door latch, she paused. The gap between door and frame allowed voices from the kitchen to be clearly heard and while she wouldn't normally eavesdrop, her purpose in being at the holding almost necessitated it.

"Stasya didn't find out from me!"

"Then why another bard only ten days later? She suspects something, Vree. I noticed. You noticed. Hanya noticed."

"You think Stasya sent her?"

"I think Stasya might have said something that aroused suspicions."

"And she's here to confirm them."

Gyhard's laugh held no humor. "Seems like."

"We *can't* let that happen."

"Vree…"

"I can be subtle."

"You're as subtle as a knife in the dark."

"That's subtle."

"Not really, love." *That* laugh held humor, Evicka realized. He found the prospect of her death funny.

She had to leave. But if she left immediately, they'd know she was on to them and that would be the end of subtle. Under the hand clutching the bathsheet, she could feel her heart slamming against her ribs. Also, she was naked. She needed her clothes. And a reason to leave before dark…

No, there wasn't a reason. She'd have to stay until morning. She'd stay awake all night, stay down in the kitchen in the light, tell them she was writing a song. She was a bard, she could make them believe it.

But first she had to let the Bardic Captain know he was right.

No. First she had to face Vree and Gyhard in the kitchen and lie through her teeth.

Deep breath.

Plastering on a smile, Evicka opened the door.

They both turned at the sound. Gyhard grinned, stood, and spread his hands. "Sorry about the lack of clothes. They were damp so Hanya hung them to dry them by the fire."

As he left the room, Vree hitched one hip up onto the edge of the table and crossed her arms.

Evicka felt her smile waver. "I need to let the Bardic Hall know I'm here safely."

"Of course."

She stepped forward and stopped as Vree's brows rose. "Like that?"

In a bathsheet. No, not like that.

But by the time she had her clothes on, the kitchen was full; Hanya and Pjason and Merlyn and Donal all talking at once, all asking her questions and telling her stories and keeping her from going outside to call the kigh without making the kind of a fuss that would give her away. Across the kitchen, Vree watched, amused. The way a cat watched a mouse, Evicka realized, the tilt to her eyes adding to the resemblance.

They were keeping her from Vree and Gyhard. Running interference every time she tried to engage with either of them. Answering her questions with questions of their own.

After eating they wanted her to sing. Stasya had Sung them the mourning and the coronation but Stasya had gotten it from the kigh, she hadn't actually been there. Perhaps a first person Recall would remind everyone where their loyalties lay.

When she finished, Vree nodded from her place by Gyhard's side. "His majesty was kinder to us than he needed to be."

And now he was dead, they could make their move.

When Evicka suggested she'd stay up and write in the kitchen, they laughed, gave her a lantern, and told her she could write in the privacy of her own room.

"This place is bigger than the six of us need," Hanya said, leading her up the stairs, "but that'll change soon."

"More people are coming?"

She stumbled and changed the subject. "Vree and Ghyard, they offered me a place when I left my husband. He was a violent ass and I walked away with only the clothes on my back. I had no other family, didn't know where to go or what to do but Ghyard was in Janinton at the mill and said they had space and needed folk not afraid of working—although they mostly needed people not afraid of cooking as it turned out but the Circle knows I can do that. I met Pjason here and hit it right off. Donal's his brother. They come from Ohrid. Eight and nine in a family what could give them nothing but good wishes. Merlyn, he killed a guy in a drunken brawl. Didn't meant to but dead's dead. He was chained to the crew building the road into Janiton for five years then they let him go. No one else would give him a chance. Do you hear what I'm saying, bard?"

That Gyhard took in the desperate and wrapped them in chains of obligation.

"I hear you."

"Good. This is your room. Stasya uses it so it's kind of the bard room. Room next to it is empty so don't worry much about noise."

A bed piled high with quilts, a chair, hooks on the wall opposite the window…Placing the lantern where the light wouldn't spill out, Evicka pulled back the heavy, wool blanket covering the shutters. No glass, not this far out, and it looked like the shutters hadn't been opened since Third Quarter. She eased one a little way, heard it creak, and froze barely breathing.

After a moment, she heard the soft hum of voices.

Not from the next room, but the room after. Mouth to the crack, she drew in a lungful of cold air and hummed the four notes to call a kigh. Not one strong enough to get all the way to Kovar, that needed volume, but one that would help her hear what was being said…as long as the pounding of her heart didn't drown it out.

"It doesn't matter what she suspects, as long as she doesn't *know*." Gyhard's tone worked to keep his blade of Jiir sheathed.

"If she Sings up a kigh, they'll tell her."

Tell her what Stasya suspected? Or tell her what was going on? The kigh she'd already Sung was no help at all.

"Vree, even if we stop her from calling a kigh while she's in the holding, she'll Sing one up as soon as she's out of sight."

"That doesn't matter. As long as she doesn't *know;* the bards won't act on mere suspicion. We just need to keep her from finding out before she leaves."

"She's afraid of you." Gyhard sounded as if that upset him. If his plan required Vree to look like something other than what she was, it was doomed to fail. That was almost reassuring.

"I noticed." Vree, however, stated a fact. People were afraid of her. It didn't bother her, it was just how it was. Evicka shivered.

❦

Morning came only because morning always did. Even with the chair up against the door, Evicak had barely slept. Would've sworn she hadn't slept at all except she'd closed her eyes in darkness and opened them at dawn. She slipped downstairs, hoping she could get packed and away before anyone woke only to find Vree in the kitchen building up the fire.

A piece of kindling in her hand—a piece of kindling Evicka had no doubt she could use as a deadly weapon—the ex-assassin raised her head and locked eyes with the bard. "Leaving without saying goodbye?"

"No." Because sneaking out would be admitting she knew and if they thought she *knew* they'd stop her. "Of course not." Even to her own ears, Evicka's laugh sounded false. "My clothes are still spread all over. I thought I should get them packed before they were even more in the way. Than they were. Last night."

Vree merely nodded and continued to watch, predator patient, as Evicka scooped trousers and sweaters and underwear off drying racks and rolled them into her pack. She could feel the other woman's gaze like a warm weight against the back of her neck.

By the time she'd slipped the strings on her harp and carefully stowed both it and her flute, the others were up and there was a pot of tea on the table and it might have been any morning in any holding since she'd left the Citadel except for the way Vree's attention never wavered. It reminded her of a dog guarding its territory and that was a horrible thing to think about another person, but once it was in her head she couldn't shake it. Somehow, she managed to eat two pieces of toast. Vree had very little more. Why weigh herself down in case she needed to kill someone.

"Are you sure you have to go so soon?" Gyhard asked an interminable time later as the two of them walked her across the stockade to the gate.

"Nothing's falling from the sky." Evicka waved at the arc of blue with one pole. "This time of the year, I need to take advantage of that."

It sounded so normal except under his words she could hear *Get out!* And under hers, nothing—all subtext deliberately erased.

Vree remained silent, her teeth clenched, a muscle jumping in her jaw.

"You're heading to Janinton next?"

"That's right." She bent to strap on her skies.

"Be best to follow the river. Ice'll be solid for a week or two yet but given the freeze/thaw we've been having, I wouldn't trust a more direct route."

"Good advice, thanks."

Words. Words. Words. Meaningless words.

"Smooth roads, Evicka." He held out his fist.

He'd washed the blood off yesterday. She could still see it but she touched her fist to his. "Be safe."

Vree kept her hands to herself although Evicka saw they'd curled into fists anyway.

The snow scraped against her skis, her weight barely cutting a visible track. There'd been a freeze in the night but by the time the sun had been up for a few hours the surface, at least, would start to soften again. As she approached the end of the valley, she whistled up a kigh and sent it back to the holding. One of the men watched from the top of the stockade. Gyhard? Or Dolan with his longbow? What was the range on a longbow? She had no idea so she concentrated on gaining as much distance as quickly as possible. It wasn't until she went around the first bend at the end of the valley that the itch between her shoulder blades began to ease.

"Although he couldn't shoot through the pack, you idiot." If her laugh held a faint hint of hysteria, it was easy enough to ignore.

Without slowing, she scanned the right bank for a way up and out of the gully to a high point of land. Following the loops of the river would add a day, maybe two to the trip. She didn't know why Gyhard wanted to delay her—well, not the specifics anyway—but she'd strike out cross country the first chance she got.

Right after she sent a kigh to the Bardic Captain.

"…the bards won't act on mere suspicion."

They didn't know the captain had only wanted confirmation of suspicions he already had. Vree might not be as much under Gyhard's control as the Bardic Captain had feared, but the two of them were definitely planning to act against the security of Shkoder.

A light rain began to fall as she skied and she was thoroughly damp again before she saw a slope gentle enough to climb. At that, *gentle enough* was bardic in description. It wasn't a steep slope but it seemed to go on forever. Her thighs were trembling when she reached the top and she paused for a moment before calling the kigh. Squinting back the way she'd come, she thought she could see into the valley, although the mist made it hard to pick out details. She felt as though she were on the battlements, guarding the rest of Shkoder from Gyhard i'Stevana and the blade he wielded.

When her lungs finally stopped burning, she licked the rain off her lips, took a deep breath, and allowed the notes to ring out pure and loud. She was too far from the holding for it to matter even if they could hear her; it was more important now to call a kigh strong enough to get back to the Bardic Hall as quickly as possible.

She had to brace herself to keep from being blown backwards, the rain making the kigh pissy and harder to control. Moving back from the edge of the bank, she added three notes for water. With so much water in the air, evoking both might help calm it long enough to hear the message she needed it to carry.

You were right. Send reinforcements.

The kigh disappeared down toward the river as she Sang the first of the four notes that would send it to the Bardic Captain. She could still feel it though. It was just playing. As she Sang the second note, it came up through the snow at her feet.

Through the snow? That was diff…

A crack opened under her right ski.

The bank collapsed.

The world disappeared in a roar of white.

She hadn't known white could roar.

She'd been dreaming about flying but the blankets were wrapped around her so tightly they kept bringing her back to earth. She could only move the fingers of her left hand no matter how much she struggled and something tickled the right side of her neck. Annoyed by the tickling, she forced herself to wake.

Wherever she was, it was dark.

Really dark.

Evicka wriggled the fingers of her left hand again.

Realized her fingers were tickling her neck.

She had her head face down in the crook of her left elbow, left hand cupped awkwardly back around her jaw. Her right arm was stretched out to the side, extended to the point where her shoulder ached. Folded at the waist, legs up and in front of her, it felt as though she was sitting on nothing at all.

She could hear the pounding of her heart.

The rasp of air moving in and out through her nose.

It wasn't the edge of blankets pressed against her throat but a hard line, a painful line. She tried to move away from it. Her head pressed back against a familiar shape. The edge of her harp case.

Her pack had twisted around and was pressing down against her head and right shoulder.

Think, Evicka!

The bank had collapsed.

She was buried in the snow, face down in an air pocket created by the angle of her arm, protected by her pack.

She touched snow with her tongue.

And not a very big air pocket.

It wouldn't last long. She'd suffocate before she froze to death…

…although she hadn't been cold until she thought of freezing to death.

She'd counted two hundred and seventeen breaths pulled carefully past the pain in her throat when she realized the air hadn't grown stale.

If the snow was porous enough air could get through…

With breath number two hundred and eighteen, she called the kigh.

Tried to call the kigh.

Breath enough to keep her alive wasn't breath enough to whistle.

Or Sing.

Or panic.

When she woke again, the snow had melted beneath her cheek. Swallowing put the pain of breathing into perspective. It might be better not to drink, to die faster rather than slower, but she drank the water pooled in the depression anyway.

Who died at twenty-two?

She tried to wriggle her feet—maybe they were sticking up out of the snow—but she couldn't move them. She couldn't move anything but the fingers of her left hand and her face.

If she could bend her hand around, work her flute case out of her pack, she might find enough air to play.

Her fingernails scraped against the oiled canvas.

Shit. She'd lost her mitten.

They'd have to find it when they dug her out. She loved those mittens.

Five hundred and twelve breaths.

Another drink.

Had Gyhard trapped the banks along the river? Told her not to leave the river knowing she would? Set this up to stop her from telling everyone his plans?

She didn't know his plans.

They knew she was suspicious. Therefore there was something for her to be suspicious of.

Three hundred in. Three hundred out. Reassuring that came out even.

Would the kigh notice when she died? Would anyone ever know?

Still not enough breath to whistle.

Four notes hummed. Nothing. Maybe because it took six breaths to do it.

She had to pee.

Warmer than snow. Could she melt her way out?

Breath enough to keep her alive wasn't enough to laugh…

…hysterically.

She was thirsty when she opened her eyes. How much time had passed? Enough melt under her cheek she could nudge her head around now and bite at the snow.

Could she eat her way out? It hurt to swallow. Hurt more? Ice an impact to keep it from swelling. Well, she'd done that. She giggled. Choked. Coughed. What dripped out her nose was too warm to be water.

A sound she didn't make. Three sounds. Crack. Slither. Thud. Temperatures drop at night. Water freezes. Ice expands. Breaks off.

If there was water in the snow…

Snow was water.

She Sang water stronger than air.

Breathe in three times. Hum.

Again.

Again.

Nothing changed.

Breathe twenty times.

Was it lighter? Her eyes were dry. Harder to get them open.

She could hear hissing. Thousands of tiny snakes?

Rain.

Water under her cheek. Hurt too much to swallow. Except for her throat, the sharp lines of pain had dulled to aches. Not good, she suspected.

Suspicious.

Gyhard i'Stevana is a multiple murderer who was pardoned against my advice.

I only know what the songs say.

I heard a few folk headed out there. You know, ones at loose ends.

This place is bigger than the six of us need, but that'll change soon.

A sudden jerk and the sharp lines of pain were back but she could move the fingers of her right hand. Not in air. In water. The slide had plunged through the ice or the river had washed away the bottom of the slide.

Breathe in three times.

Hum through her nose. Higher pitched and easier to hear.

Again.

Again.

Who died at twenty-two? Tragic heroes.

There'd be a song. It'd be sad. Of course it'd be sad. She was dead. Who'd write it?

Alone. Alone. So far from home. Songs crushed…

What rhymed with crushed? Mushed? Rushed? Pushed?

Same letters. Wrong sound. That was stupid. Who decided how words were spelled?

If she'd managed to send the kigh to the Bardic Captain before the bank collapsed, she'd be a hero. Still dead though.

Thirty-one, thirty-two, twenty-seven…she kept losing count. She'd have to start over. Maybe she'd leave her eyes closed. She couldn't move her right fingers anymore. Hardly surprising given the temperature of the water.

She could Sing fire. Not now. But she could. Fire was warm.

She wasn't actually cold.

That definitely wasn't good.

Sixteen. Seventeen. Seventeen. Seventeen. What came after seventeen?

"Because it was a water kigh! Start in the river and work your way up!"

Eighteen!

Warm…something…closed around her hand.

"I've got her! There's a pulse! She's alive!"

Good.

"Okay, the angle…her shoulder has to be here. Head's here then! Vree, get down!"

What was Gyhard planning out here in the wild?

"I'm still the lightest. We don't want to compact the snow."

"What do you know about snow?"

Good question. The assassin and her brother were from the empire's southern province.

"More than I want to."

Good answer.

She could hear scrabbling. Scrambling. Scribbling. No, that wasn't right...

Light. Good thing she had her eyes closed.

"Doesn't look good." Sounded like the older man. Started with an em. If it was important she'd remember it later.

"Evicka? Can you hear me?"

Warmth against her cheek, then pressing gently against the back of her neck. Then what felt like a hundred tiny fingers going through her hair.

"Why is her hair moving?" Hanya. She remembered Hanya.

"Kigh. They couldn't get to her."

"Shouldn't they have gone for help?"

"They don't do much without being told. Get her legs uncovered while I move the pole off her throat."

"If she loses her voice..."

That would be bad, but breathing was good too. An ethereal touch against her lips. Between her lips. Air that tasted of spring...

She opened her eyes to see Vree bending over her, holding a long knife. "Don't talk. You haven't broken your neck so I'm cutting the pack free. We can ease you back at a better angle."

"Not...healer."

"No, but killing teaches you a lot about what works and what doesn't. And what part of don't talk don't you understand?" She muttered, *bards*. The knife flashed.

Evika felt a sudden easing of pressure and a relief of specific pain amid the general. Then different pain. Lots of it. She choked. Coughed until another touch against her lips calmed her. "Dy...ing."

Vree nodded. "Maybe. But you were in good condition. You might make it."

"Tell...me."

"What?"

Another sip of air. "What...can't they...know?"

"Drop it."

"Last...re...quest."

This time when Vree said *bards* it sounded like profanity. "I'm with child. His child. Gyhard's child," she added, although Evicka had assumed as much. "If the bards find out they'll tell Bannon before I can and you don't want that."

"*You* don't want that," Gyhard said from somewhere near.

"Neither do you," Vree told him shortly.

"That's...all?"

Vree turned her attention back to Evicka. "All? That's..." Evicka watched her visibly struggling for the words. Her willingness to expose that kind of vulnerability defined how big this was. "That's likely to get people killed if we don't tell my brother the right way. Now shut up."

She knew what Gyhard had been up to. Wait until the Bardic Captain found out. Giggling hurt.

A shadow and the em man appeared. Disappeared. "Throat's badly bruised."

Vree frowned. "I'm more worried about fingers and toes."

"Vree." Gyhard used the tone healers used when they said, *We've lost her.* She wasn't lost. She was found. She wanted to turn her head when Vree did but couldn't.

"Can we move it?"

"Not without a block and tackle and she won't live that long. Only the cold and the angle have kept her from bleeding to death already."

That really didn't sound good.

"Then we cut them off."

Them?

"You can't just…"

Vree cut Hanya off. "Or she dies."

"When Donal brings the healer from Janinton…"

"She'll be dead before Donal gets back."

"But to cut off her legs!" That was Hanya's man. Pja-something. They were all here. Except Donal. That was nice.

"Or she dies," Vree repeated. She wrapped the hand not holding the knife around Evicka's chin. "It's your choice, bard."

"Vree."

"She's aware, Gyhard. It's her life."

Evicka could hear Vree and the healer talking in the hall. The tone of Vree's response suggested the healer had been giving advice about the pregnancy with no idea of how lucky she was that Vree had stopped killing people. A glance to where the blankets lay flat against the bed. Still good with a knife though.

Half a dozen kigh came in through the open window, circled the room and left. Now that Stasya and Annice were only a few hours out, they'd started to calm but they'd been more trouble than they were worth from the moment she'd been found. Every bard in Shkoder—and Karlene who was halfway between

Shkoder and the empire—had checked in on her. The captain had been so invasive, Evicka had finally sent a kigh to Tadeus begging him to intervene.

Tadeus understood. Blind since birth, he'd spent his life teaching people to see him, rather than what they saw as his disability.

She was rubbing the top of her right thigh—the handspan remaining—when Vree knocked and came into the room. The ex-assassin had been surprisingly comforting. Blunt, but not cruel. If Hanya's arms had provided a warm circle to weep in, Vree's company had eventually stopped the tears because Vree treated her like a bard—like an annoyance inevitable when living in Shkoder.

"The healer tells me you'll regain the sensitivity in your fingers."

The healer had just removed the mittens stuffed with paste that smelled of cardamon. Evicka hoped the smell would fade. "She doesn't think she can save my toes though."

Vree actually snickered and Evicka grinned. The tip of her nose was still numb, but she'd been promised feeling would return to that as well. Grin fading, she patted the side of the bed. "If we're going to talk, we need to do it now. Once Stasya and Annice get here…"

"No one will get a word in edgewise." Vree sat, her condition still hidden behind bulky sweaters even though spring had finally come to Bicaz. She sat where Evicka's legs would have been—the only one in the holding who did. The others treated the space as though Evicka maintained a claim to it. Vree treated it like an empty part of the bed. "So, talk."

"The Bardic Captain sent me here because he doesn't trust Gyhard."

"He trusts me?"

"He thinks Gyhard controls you."

Vree snorted. "I've met Kovar. He doesn't think, he reacts. He finds what Gyhard did to survive abhorrent and everything builds on that. He feels sorry for me…" She raised a hand when Evicka opened her mouth. "He objects to how assassins are trained. Because of this, he can't believe I could willingly…" Cheeks suddenly flushed, she ran a hand through her hair.

"Love?" Evicka asked, amused.

"…make a life with Gyhard. He sees the knife but never stops to consider the person holding it."

Kovar saw Vree as the knife and an abomination holding it, but Evicka understood what Vree meant. "He hears one note and believes he knows the whole song."

"If you have to get bardic about it."

"You don't mind?"

"That you get bardic?" She grinned as Evicka stuck out her tongue but sobered immediately. "That you followed the orders of your captain? I spent most of my life following orders. That Gyhard and I are considered dangerous? That's fact. That Kovar is the wrong person to command the most powerful force in Shkoder? That, I mind."

"The bards aren't," Evicka began but trailed off under Vree's level gaze. She could see how it looked to an outsider but the bards weren't a powerful force, they were the eyes and ears of Shkoder.

When she told that to Vree, the assassin raised a brow. "Your captain's words? Seems like something's missing."

Before Evicka could explain, half a dozen kigh roared in through the window and nearly shoved Vree off the bed. Stasya and Annice had arrived.

***

Stasya accompanied her as far as Vidor, the two of them Singing strong enough water to tame even a First Quarter river. They shot the rapids just above Janinton in a channel of kigh then pried the healer's grip from the gunnels and dropped her off, muttering about bards and insanity—a huge improvement on previous muttering about infection and scarring.

At Vidor, Stasya handed her off to Tadeus and the two of them took the riverboats toward Elbasan. River inns had their own docks and the boatmen vied to carry her in from the water. Usually because they thought it would net them a chance with Tadeus. Once or twice because they thought it would net them a chance with her. She wasn't ready for that yet, but it was good to know that someday she could be. Tadeus played every night for appreciative crowds while Evicka Sang a few harmonies but mostly wove her flute around his harp and voice. At the Rivermaiden, when the crowd called for *Assassin's Love Song*, he grinned and handed her his harp.

Walking would have to be redefined, but the crowd's reaction let her know she hadn't lost any of what made her a bard—although that night she cried in Tadeus' arms for what she *had* lost.

Pjasef met them in Riverton with a wheeled chair.

"I had my father add straps here for your flute and here..." He spun the chair to show her. "...for your harp. This is the light one, for getting around the city and the Citadel, but he's working on one that'll take the weight of a pack. He figures he can make a small donkey cart you could get in and out of on your own with the chair hooked low on the back so you could still Walk anywhere the roads go. Uh..." He leaned closer to Tadeus. "Why is she crying?"

She punched him in the thigh. "Because you heard the whole song, you ass!"

That night they wrote another verse.

Nine months and three days after she left, Evicka returned to the Citadel.

Marija was back on the gate. She frowned, pushed her hair off her face, and said, "I can't put my finger on it, but there's something different about you."

As the gate guards looked everywhere but at the two of them, Evicka rolled over her foot.

When she finished cursing, Marija cupped the younger bard's face in both hands, bent, and kissed her gently. "I'm glad you're not dead."

"Most of the time, so am I." No point in lying.

"Come find me in the dark times. We'll get drunk and make up embarrassing songs about men we've slept with."

Behind her, one of the guards made a sound that might have been a protest.

The Citadel courtyard was nearly empty—a page charging across at full speed, two courtiers hurrying in the opposite direction, their heads together, the Bardic Captain waiting by the entrance to the Bardic Hall. Evicka took a deep breath and wheeled toward him.

Nine months and three days. She thought of Vree. Nine months and three days was long enough to build a whole new person.

"Why isn't Pjasef…"

"Pjasef delivered the chair. He didn't need to deliver me."

"Yes. Of course. As you mean to go on…" The captain rubbed his hands together, clearly distressed. "I sent you there. I sent you to them. She cut off your legs…"

"To save my life. She wasn't torturing me at Gyhard's command." No surprise really when the captain didn't see the humor. Evicka sighed. "If this had happened anywhere else, I'd have died. If Vree hadn't seen the kigh…"

"She sees *kigh*?" The captain had probably been fifteen the last time he'd hit that note.

The water kigh Evicka had Sung had gone off with some urgency but no direction. "She saw water running against the current."

"That's not…"

"She notices things."

"Of course. Her training." Evicka could see him thinking of how Gyhard could use that training but he visibly shook it off and bent to touch her lightly on the shoulder. "I am so sorry."

It wasn't sympathy. Well, it *was* sympathy but it was mostly apology.

"I failed you," he continued. "I am responsible for the bards as the bards are responsible for Shkoder."

Evicka had Recalled the death of King Theron and the coronation of Queen Onele all the way to Bicaz. She wondered what they'd think of that.

"The healers have said they want to see you."

Of course. "Before or after my Recall?"

"Your Recall?" All bards returning from a Walk gave their Recall first to the captain and then a more detailed version to a scribe. Except, apparently, bards without legs.

She looked at him the way Vree had looked at her.

He cleared his throat. "I'll take your Recall when they're done."

Evicka looked pointedly at the broad stone steps leading up into the Bardic Hall. The captain flushed. He hadn't yet glanced below her waist and he didn't now.

"We can use the library. It's on the first floor and there are doors leading out into the gardens. We'll have to build a ramp and my office...I'll have to move my office...You can teach, of course. Let me assure you, Evicka, there will always be a place for you in the Bardic Hall."

"Because I'm a bard."

He looked confused and she suddenly felt very tired.

"I'll go see the healers now, Captain." She pulled at the cuffs of her leather gloves—Tadeus had given her three pairs declaring she couldn't possibly wear black every day—and rolled back, giving herself space to turn. A bit of breeze lifted her hair and she thought she heard Vree say, *"Seems like something's missing."* The captain wanted the bards to be the eyes and ears of Shkoder. Who then was the voice? "Captain?"

"Yes?" His gaze skittered past her.

No. She needed to think about it a bit longer. "I'll send a kigh if they're going to be long."

Evicka could feel people watching her from the windows, but that was hardly surprising. People always watched bards.

Bone Garden

AMANDA DOWNUM

They found the girl on the back doorstep an hour before dawn. Gentian might have mistaken her for a pile of rags in the dim glow of the streetlamps but for the hair spilling like dark water down the steps and the pale hand curling against icy stones.

He drew up sharply, breath catching; Val stumbled into his back. Stories of a dozen murdered women crowded his head, driving away his pleasant drunken abstraction.

"What is it?" Val muttered. "Oh—" His hand tightened on Gentian's elbow.

Gentian scanned the empty street behind them: shops closed, windows shuttered against the cold, frost-slick cobbles glazed with lamplight. Laughter and voices carried from the next block, but the alley behind the Orpheum Rhodon was silent.

He and Val exchanged a glance. They'd had a crowd a few hours ago, all their friends and as many strangers staggering through the Garden to celebrate the Rhodon's smash opening of *Mirror of Dreams*. But time and wine felled their companions one by one, till they were left to wander back to the theatre by themselves.

If not a murder, it might be a trap, but they stood and gaped like idiots and no one emerged from the shadows to rob them. The girl didn't move.

"Is she—" Val swallowed, his fingers still digging into Gentian's arm. He made no move to find out.

Gentian sighed, his breath a shimmering plume in the darkness, and knelt to check her pulse; his own beat sharp in his throat. He hadn't touched a corpse since he'd been the one to find his grandmother— Bile rose in his throat and he swallowed. Her wrist was icy and fragile between his fingers, but her pulse was a steady throb. Relief nearly cost him his dinner and subsequent bottles of wine anyway. He sat down hard on the steps.

But if she wasn't dead, why was she here? She looked too tattered and threadbare for the usual clientele. He couldn't smell alcohol or opium on her, nor find any wound. The bones in her hands were sharp as the sticks of a fan.

Cold stone leeched the warmth out of him, leaving tired sobriety in its place. "We can't leave her here," he said, rubbing his face. Stage makeup he never got around to washing off left pale residue on his fingers. "Elisa would have a fit." And besides, it was snowing again, fat flakes drifting past his nose to snag and melt in the girl's tangled hair.

Val unlocked the door and crouched beside them, sorting through the mess of skirts and scarves until Gentian had his hands under her arms and Val had her legs. Too thin, but long-boned and limp; they cursed and stumbled over the threshold and into the warmer darkness of the hall. As quiet inside as out—plenty of other actors and crew lived in the Rhodon, waiting for money or patronage to find rooms of their own, but they were still carousing or passed out drunk.

"What are we doing with her, anyway?" Val asked.

With a few awkward turns, they maneuvered her into one of the backstage waiting rooms. One of those where over-eager patrons might claim a tryst—a lock on the door and worn velvet upholstery, flaking gilt candelabras and stained-glass lamps. Like everywhere backstage, the air smelled of sawdust and face-paint, sweat and perfume and mineral oil. Gentian barked his shin against a chair as they set their burden down and cursed, while Val fumbled his way across the room to strike a light. Tugging his scarves away from his throat—ever since the first bite of winter, Elisa wouldn't let any of her singers out of the building with bare necks—Gentian knelt to examine his charge in the amber spill of lamplight.

Her skin was as fair as his instead of Selafaïn brown or bronze, her face a long oval beneath tangled winter-brown hair. Familiarity nagged at him, but perhaps it was only the coloring. Hundreds of Rosian refugees had come to Erisín in the last ten years, perhaps thousands by now.

Dozens had died since autumn, more than the usual toll of hunger and disease. At least five young women had been murdered by a bloodthirsty slasher—a demon, rumor claimed—and more were killed in the riots that sprang up in the wake of those murders. It wasn't a good time to be Rosian in Oldtown. Or anywhere.

Looking closer, he frowned—blood streaked the girl's cheeks like tears, crusted rust-red in dark lashes. He touched her head lightly, searching again for a wound, but found nothing. Gentian swallowed: it was the mark of an oracle amongst his people. He doubted anyone else in the theatre would recognize it, but he licked the edge of a scarf and hastily scrubbed the blood away. Oracles weren't demons, but it was hard to explain the difference. Her blue fingertips were a more pressing concern, anyway.

Val leaned over his shoulder—stumbled and leaned on it; the smell of wine clung to him thick as perfume. "Now what?"

"Either she wakes up and we find out what happened, or..." Gentian rubbed his face again, contemplating the nuisance of charity. "I suppose she can have my bed, otherwise. I'll sleep with you."

Val snorted. "You snore and take all the covers. Sleep with her instead."

"Maybe I can steal a jacket from costumes," Gentian said, frowning at her threadbare coat. Her shoes were cracked, stockings too thin for the weather; if nothing else he could give her a better pair of socks.

And why, he asked himself, did he care? He could find a carriage and have her taken to a shelter for less trouble. She was Rosian, clearly a refugee—everything he had distanced himself from. But so familiar. He brushed her hair away from her face.

Thick arching brows, a long hooked nose, cheekbones very like his own. A solitary pox-scar dented her brow, in the center where temples marked their priests. Gentian's breath caught as familiarity deepened into realization. Taller and thinner than the girl he remembered, but....

She stirred, eyes opening—deep and dark, and the bottom fell out of his stomach. Chapped lips cracked as she smiled. Before he could stop her, she spoke.

"Kostya!"

He winced at the name he hadn't used in years. "Sonya." His hand shook as he reached for her, half expecting her to be insubstantial as a phantom now, a vengeful spectre sent to remind him of his sins. The chill starkness of her flesh didn't reassure him.

Behind them, Val made a curious noise. Sonya glanced up and stiffened, wary as an animal.

"This is Valerian. He's a friend. Val, this is Sonya—my cousin."

"What are you doing here?" Gentian asked after Val had gone to bed and he'd dragged Sonya into a warm bath. Steam fogged the narrow window and the faint metallic smell of tap water filled the room. Her clothes lay in a heap on the tiles—better off in the furnace than the laundry. "It's not safe out there alone."

"Safe as anywhere. I was waiting for you." Still too pale, but at least she wasn't blue anymore. She sorted through soaps and bath salts, opening a bottle and sniffing before replacing the stopper. The next she sprinkled into the water. "I missed you after the show."

"You were here?"

"Of course. It was wonderful." She selected another soap and began scrubbing her hair. "The costumes, the songs… The moving statues were very clever. But Lucretia's maid needs to work on her timing."

"We've told her." Shame warmed his neck, and not for Silvia's timing. He hadn't thought to invite Sonya. Hadn't thought of her in so long. Had tried so hard to wipe away the past, while she and the rest of their family clung to it.

"I'm sorry," he said softly.

She raised her eyebrows, soapsuds dripping down one cheek. "She wasn't that bad." Her lips curled, and he knew she understood him. Of course she did—his best friend since they could walk, as close as any sister. Closer still, perhaps, if not for clan consanguinity laws.

He remembered the blood on her face and swallowed. "Sonya—" He knelt beside the lacquered wooden tub, soaking the knees of his trousers. The smell of sea salt and citrus drifted off the water, off her skin. "When I found you"—he lowered his voice, glancing over his shoulder to double-check the latch—"you had the ašara." The red tears.

Her face greyed. She sank into the water without answering, hair snaking around her like kelp and a cloud of suds spreading across the surface. Like Ophelia in *Undine*, frozen in her lake. He wished he knew how to recreate the image on stage.

She rose just as he began to wonder if she'd passed out again, blowing water off her lips and raking wet hair out of her eyes. "Thank you," she said, "for the bath. I haven't had a proper one in weeks."

He remembered the plumbing, or lack thereof, in Little Kiva too well—Cabbagetown, the refugee quarter was more often called. He remembered all of it, though he'd spent the last five years scrubbing Ashke Ros out of his voice and mannerisms, answering questions about his past with vagaries and the occasional lie. Dodging the question the way Sonya dodged his now.

"Sonya."

"I know." She drew her legs up, resting her forehead on her knees. Her hair clung to her shoulders and arms, bronze on ivory, leaking shining rivulets down her skin. Gooseflesh roughened her arms; the tub had cooled and steam dripped down the windowpane. The sky beyond pearled with coming dawn. "It took me while I was waiting for you. The sight. I saw... The houses all around, the people in them. The things they do." She turned her face to him, and her eyes were black wells. "The things you did?"

And still do. "You know where we are. You know who I am."

"Kostya—"

"Gentian."

Her lips twisted. "The program said Ikarus Gentius."

"I couldn't be Gentian on stage—what if I turned out famous? The Rose Council will want the name back eventually." And of course he couldn't use his real name, not if he was pretending to be something besides immigrant trash. "But I'm still Gentian for now."

The look she gave him held neither disapproval nor condemnation, but a sadness that cut deeper still. "Even to me?"

He rocked back on his heels and stood. "It's who I am."

"You can't be an actor without being a prostitute?" She only stumbled a little on the word.

"Prostitutes make more money. And you're changing the subject." He searched the cabinets for clean towels. "We left the veštimi behind. There are no oracles here." His hands tightened in folded linen. "Are there?"

They had dreamed of many things as children, but more than anything Sonya had wanted the ašara and the oracle's veil. None of that childhood joy was in her face now. "We left the veštimi behind, but there are others."

Other spirits: the thought made his skin crawl. Erisín was a haunted city, and its specters were hungry.

"I—" Sonya swallowed, and Gentian hid a frown. He remembered her poise, her calm in the face of any horror. The Sonya he knew never hid from questions, or things that needed saying. That Sonya was never afraid to meet his gaze. "I need help," she finished in a whisper. "Can I stay with you tonight?"

She reached for the clay pitcher beside the tub to rinse the last of the soap from her hair. Her hand shook too badly, and the handle slipped from her grasp. Gentian caught it before it shattered on the floor.

"Of course you can stay. Get out of there before you freeze again. We'll talk in the morning." The afternoon, now.

She rose, reaching for the offered towel with a wrinkled hand. "Thank you." He wasn't sure if she meant it for the bed or the reprieve.

His room was in its usual disarray—costumes and clothes draped across the bed and chair, makeup scattered across the desk. Vials and cases had been shoved aside to make room for flowers. He grinned at the sight, leaning close to breathe in the heady scent. Roses mostly, red and white and violet, cloying in their profusion. A few clusters of blue gentians, the best of which someone had put in a bowl of water. A scattering of the wildflower bunches sold for a penny in the lobby. Greenhouses and herbal alchemists loved the theatre. There were letters, too, buried beneath the flowers; he was sure some of them held lucrative offers.

"Oh." Sonya's eyes widened. "Is it always like this?" She looked from the flowers to the scattered clothes, playbills tacked to the walls, charms hanging from the ceiling and the window frame. A series of charcoal sketches a besotted art student had given him. A syrinx he'd found in a park and kept, though he hadn't the patience to learn it.

He chuckled. "Messy? Yes. If you mean the flowers, this was the first time I had more than an extra's part. I wouldn't mind if this kept up, though."

"This isn't what I imagined," she said, sitting cautiously on the edge of the narrow bed.

"You thought of gilt and velvet? Candles and incense?" Her cheeks darkened. "Those are downstairs."

He crouched to light the brazier; the chill wasn't bad with the shutters and curtains drawn, but Sonya shivered in her damp towels. Light and heat leaked through the filigreed brass, painting golden patterns over the dusty floor. He rummaged a nightshirt from the clothing chest.

"Do you need anything else? I'll find you something else to wear in the morning—afternoon."

"No, thank you." She unwound the towel from her head, long dark hair spilling over her shoulders. "Will you stay with me?"

The smell of salt and oranges and clean girl wafted around him, heavy with memories. The shores of the Zaratan Sea, where he and Sonya and their friends waded and splashed and looked for amber. And a day in Erisín years later, when the two of them left the city and climbed down the rocky cliffs to the bay to watch the cold water churn against barnacled rocks. Sonya had teased the little red crabs that lurked in tide pools and waved to passing ships, her braid unraveling in the wind. They'd eaten bread and oranges on the rocks, and everything smelled of salt and citrus. She tasted of it when they kissed.

Not their first kiss, but the first one that lingered too long. The first one that felt like falling, like missing a stair in the dark.

Gentian swallowed, the past catching in his dry throat. The memory of that kiss was strong enough to startle him. But she wasn't that girl anymore; he wasn't that boy. He didn't know who they were to each other now. "I shouldn't," he said. "You need rest, and I snore and steal the covers." He leaned down to kiss her brow, tasting salt and skin. "I am glad to see you, Sonyushka." The Rosian nickname stumbled off his tongue, and he winced.

"You were more convincing as a magic mirror." She smiled to take the sting out, clasping his hand quickly before he pulled away. "Goodnight, Gentian."

He shut the door behind him and leaned unsteadily against the wall. He'd made a clean break when he left the refugee shanties. Never went back, never tried to contact the few of his family who still lived. Even when a note reached him two years ago, Sonya's neat handwriting telling of his mother's death, he had mourned alone. Easier for everyone, he'd told himself, by which he meant easiest for him. Now the walls he'd built between his old life and the new teetered. They would fall and crush him if he wasn't careful.

A pale flash of movement brought his head up. Siglinda stood at the end of the hall, like a ghost in her white nightdress, fair hair shining over her shoulders. One of his violinists for *Mirror*, Ilario's especial attendants—he had to look twice to be sure he had the right sister, as always. She didn't move as he walked down the hall; he had to pass her to reach Val's room.

Her green eyes met his as he drew near, pale and unnerving in the nascent light. "You've brought magic into the house," she said softly. "Dangerous magic."

He paused mid-stride. She and her sister told fortunes on the side instead of whoring—barbarian witches from the frozen north. Hard to say what was real and what was stage tricks and chicanery, but under her eerie stare he was loath to dismiss the warning.

"What should I do?" he asked.

She shrugged, her wide mouth twisting sympathetically. "Be careful." She walked away, bare feet silent on the boards, and disappeared around the corner with a dramatic flare of her skirts.

"Actors," he muttered. He felt the sunrise in his burning eyes, his dragging limbs and rasping throat. Elisa would peel his bones for props if he lost his voice. Relatives and oracles and dangerous magic would have to wait till he'd had a good day's rest.

Val was already asleep, snoring himself despite his aspersions. He didn't stir as Gentian kicked off his boots and stripped his jacket—borrowed from costuming, and he was glad he'd managed not to spill wine on it. Light soaked the curtains, pale gold as Vallish mead; his eyes felt lined with sawdust.

Val made a soft noise as Gentian crawled between him and the wall. The bed wasn't meant for two, but they were used to making do. After a fair amount of prodding, Val rolled onto his side and Gentian curled against his back.

It's who I am now, he thought, breathing in wine and warm flesh and the saffron and cedar perfume of Val's hair. He was asleep before he could convince himself it was true.

He woke to sticky heat and the smell of someone else's sweat, one elbow jammed against the wall and Val's arm draped across his stomach. Val's breath came slow and even, but when Gentian turned his head his friend's eyes were open. Black and sleepy and thick-lashed, they'd won him no end of clients.

"You never told me you had a cousin."

Gentian grimaced, rubbed his tongue against sleep-soured teeth. "You don't talk about your family. None of us do."

"My sister lives in Altarlight. I'll bring you over for dinner some day."

"My family are refugees. I'm not bringing you home. It's history."

"Your history is sleeping down the hall. Probably awake by now." Val stretched, muscles rippling under tea-colored skin, and reached out to tug open the curtain. Gentian flinched from the apricot light—afternoon by the angle. "Not everyone sleeps as late as you."

"You're one to talk."

Val grinned and pressed a quick kiss on Gentian's lips before rolling out of bed. "Get dressed. Your history's waiting."

But Sonya wasn't in his room, awake or otherwise. He swallowed nervous spit and glanced around like an idiot, as if she might have hidden herself in a chest or behind the curtains. The room still reeked of roses, a note of decay threading the sweetness. He should get the crew urchins to hang them to dry; Elisa wanted to put on *Astrophel and Satis* next season, and she could never have enough dead flowers for the sorceress's tower.

He checked the mirror—the silk was in place, just as he'd left it. Elisa paid for the best wards, but he hadn't forgotten Siglinda's warning.

He found Sonya downstairs in the theatre's narrow kitchen, sitting with Siglinda and her sister. The twins had scavenged better clothes: trousers and a blouse, a worn velvet jacket that likely came from the back of the costume closet. One of them—Siglinda—sat at the table, pouring olive oil onto a plate, while Gisela stood behind Sonya, combing out her hair. Like the mirror-twins seducing Lucretia, and Gentian paused in the doorway, a greeting dying in his throat.

"It's a local trick," Siglinda said, her voice low and amused. "You study the shapes in the oil and they show you the future. Or at least blobs that might look like something meaningful, if you squint hard enough." She reached for the bottle of vinegar; the smell cut through the usual scents of spices and old grease as red dripped into golden oil.

Sonya studied the shimmering plate and laughed. Her color was better, but Gentian didn't like the sharpness of her cheekbones. "All I see are blobs and splotches. I think I like tea leaves better."

"You have to use your imagination," Siglinda said. "That one, for instance, looks like coins. So you tell the client it means fortune, or debt. And that looks like a bloodstain—childbirth, maybe, or a betrayal. You have to get them talking first, find the clues."

"So it's all a trick?"

"It's symbolism," said Gisela. She lifted a handful of Sonya's hair and slid the comb through it. Clean and untangled, it fell past her hips. Strands of chestnut and brass gleamed among the darker length. Gentian's would be nearly that dark, if he didn't rinse it with chamomile and rhubarb and harsh alchemical concoctions. "You find the right symbols, and the querent will apply them to their life. To do more takes real magic."

She leaned over Sonya's shoulder to study the plate. "I see coins, yes, but not fortune. Those are the coins in the mouths of the dead. And the blood is for shedding and the blood that binds. Family."

Sonya laughed, but from the doorway Gentian saw her lips blanche. "I'll stick to astrology," she said, breaking off a corner of bread and dragging it through the portents. "It wastes less food."

The twins glanced up then, their eyes turning to Gentian in unison. The blue stare and the green pinned him, cool and measuring. Walking into their combined gaze felt like walking into the Dis—cold and irrevocable—but he stepped into the kitchen, smiling for Sonya as she turned toward him. Gisela laid the comb on the table.

"Thank you," Sonya said, twisting her hair into a heavy coil at the nape of her neck.

The twins drew back as Gentian approached, moving with the eerie synchronicity they practiced for hours on stage. Siglinda's gaze lingered before she turned away, and her warning echoed in his head.

"Good morning," he said, with a cheer he didn't feel. "How did you sleep?"

Her lashes lowered with her smile. "Better than I have in a long time. But morning is long gone—the bells just rang the fifth terce. Do you perform tonight?"

"Tomorrow. Tonight is *The Two Tristans*." A light farce to contrast with Mirror's tenebric madness and death. The Rhodon made sure to have a comedic troupe at hand to keep things from getting too dismal.

He reached for the bread, but was distracted by a news-sheet tucked under the plate of oil. He eased the paper free—already wrinkled and smudged by other handlers. The smeared lines shared gossip from the Azure Palace, academic quarrels in Archlight, and reviews of performances at the Magdalen and Tharymis as well as the Rhodon.

Today, they also told of death. Gentian frowned as he read of a young woman's body found outside a cemetery in Oldtown—a cemetery on the edge of Little Kiva. *Constables are investigating*, the paper said, the ink imbued with derision at the thought. In the nearby tenements of Birthgrave, several infants and elderly had died in the night. Not uncommon for the season, especially after a terrible outbreak of influenza only last month, but several exorcists had been seen investigating the buildings.

"Did you read—" Gentian broke off, looking down. Sonya's hands shook as she shredded the last of her bread into crumbs. Her mouth was a bloodless line. "Sonya, what's wrong?" An uneasy feeling uncoiled in the pit of his stomach. "Is this why you came to see me?"

Her eyes flickered around the kitchen, landing everywhere but him. Footsteps creaked overhead and he heard Elisa's voice upstairs, rousting the last of the slugabeds. The theatre staggered to life for the night.

"Can we go somewhere else?" Sonya said "Somewhere quiet."

"When did you start avoiding questions this way?"

She cocked an eyebrow. "I learned all sorts of things after you left."

Gentian sighed. "All right. There's a teashop down the street—we can sit outside."

☙❧

Bundled and layered against the chill, they followed the arc of Chloris Circle to the west. The sun rode low against the rooftops, slanting light through the clouds to pick diamonds from the dirty slush that lined the streets. The Garden's residents skirted the ice, darting from door to warm door, finishing errands before dusk brought crowds.

The Melusine was full, as it often was, but the weather left the little tables on the pavement empty. Someone clapped and whistled when Gentian drew back the hood of his coat; the applause grew as he neared the counter. He turned and sketched a flamboyant bow, ears burning with more than cold.

Sonya's reached for her purse but Gentian was faster. The young man behind the counter refused the clipped silver obol with a wink, though. Gentian winked back, and dropped a smaller coin into the tip jar. A beet-red flush rose in Sonya's cheeks. It wouldn't last, of course—favorites at the Rhodon changed as quickly as the backdrops—but Gentian meant to take advantage of the adulation while he could.

They took their tea—pale with warm milk and fragrant with cardamom and anise—and pastries outside, where the icy breeze ripped ribbons of steam off the cups.

"Now," he said, after Sonya took a bite of spiced cake. "What's wrong? What don't you want to tell me?"

She wiped cinnamon dust from the corner of her mouth. "Everything you don't want to hear."

"You can tell me anything. You always could. And I *am* glad to see you."

She sighed, long fingers folding around her cup. "Even so. You left to escape the family's demands. Knowing that, do you think it's easy to ask you for help?"

He couldn't meet her eyes, light as walnut shells in the slanting light and flecked with gold. He stared into his tea instead. Leaves swirled in the milky depths; if they had a message for him, he couldn't understand it. "I had to get out of there, but it was never you I wanted to escape."

Her eyebrows winged toward her hair. "No? You seemed a better actor than that last night."

When he was eight—when he was Kostya, and innocent—he'd told his mother he wanted to marry Sonya one day. His mother had laughed, and explained about the consanguinity laws that governed Rosian families. She showed him the records of the Ïerevny family, lovingly illuminated in red and gold and gilt, and explained why no cousins in their generation were permitted to wed. Much of it was lost on him, but he nodded solemnly and explained in turn to Sonya why they would have to remain merely cousins and friends.

Years later, after the sack of Gamayun, after the Ordozh raiders swept west across the Aden and Volhyn Ros and Sarkany began sweeping up the spoils, the last of the Ïerevny lived in one crumbling tenement in Little Kiva. Drafts blew through in the winter and midges in the summer, both bringing illness. The walls stank of pork fat and beets and cabbage, because the family clung to traditional recipes when local food would be cheaper and fresher—the way they clung to all the things that didn't matter, because everything that did was ashes behind them.

One day that fall, Kostya and Sonya returned from the bay, damp and salt-flecked and flushed from the wind and the memory of a kiss. Kostya's mother, whom he hadn't heard laugh in months, read the space between them. That night, as he chopped onions for dinner, she suggested that a marriage between cousins might bring more good than harm after all the family had lost. Kostya pretended it was the onions that made his eyes leak, but he made his decision that night.

The next morning, he left for the Garden.

"I'm sorry," he whispered, still looking into his tea.

Sonya's hand settled over his, warm from her cup. He remembered the calluses, but the bitten-down nails were new. "I understand. It was...hard to forgive, sometimes, but I always understood."

Of course she had. She always understood, always forgave, always had an answer. She was the one their mothers turned to, who the grandmothers praised. As a child he never minded, but later, after everything was in ruins, the family relied on Sonya more than ever, while he grew more lost every day.

That was history now, he told himself. It didn't matter. "What happened to you, after?"

She shrugged. "The usual, at first. I took in sewing and laundry. A few booksellers and students were interested in translations of Rosian stories, but not many. I helped our neighbors write letters of inquiry for jobs—and forged a few recommendations. It wasn't bad, for a while, until Mother got sick. I had money saved for doctors, but there was nothing they could do in the end. The last of my savings bought her coffin."

Gentian swallowed before he could speak; the tea went down bitter as char. "You could have sent for me—"

Her eyes narrowed as she looked up, anger cracking her calm veneer. She pulled her hand back. "You didn't come home for your own mother's funeral, Kostya. Why would you have come for mine? I'm sorry," she said quickly, scrubbing a hand across her face as if to wipe the words away. "I didn't come here to blame you."

"No, but I deserve it. You don't have to go back. You can stay with me. Or we'll find you a place of your own." The words spilled out fast and clumsy before he could second-guess them. "You can translate Rosian poetry and plays, or work for the Rhodon, or a teashop, or whatever you like." He leaned in, and the steam from their tea drifted damp against his burning cheeks. "Not everyone here is a prostitute, and it isn't such a bad place to live. Look."

He swept a hand eastward, toward the shop fronts and narrow houses, the chimney smoke shredding on the breeze. The sky above the jagged rooftops was streaked with rose and gold and the last light fell warm across the slate tiles, gleaming on windowpanes and gilding the marble pediment of the Rhodon where it rose above its neighbors. The sight still caught in Gentian's throat—the first place in years he'd dare call home.

"No," Sonya murmured. "Not so bad."

His hands tingled with sudden nerves. She had come to him for help after all this time. They could start over together here, without the misery of the slums—

But when he lowered his eyes she had turned away, staring down the street, her shoulders stiff beneath velvet and trailing scarves. Two men and a woman walked toward them, striding heedlessly through piled slush. Their steps and swinging arms matched with an unnerving synchronicity that reminded him of the twins. They drew up beside the table, and the woman stepped forward.

"There you are, Sonyushka. We were worried." The words were honey-sweet but her smile was cold. She wore no gloves and her throat was bare beneath the upturned collar of her coat.

"I can take care of myself," Sonya replied with equal chill. "You should know that by now."

The woman—barely that, years younger than Gentian—sparked the same sense of familiarity that he'd felt when he first saw Sonya. Blonde hair spilled from under her knit cap, windtangled ringlets framing sharp cold-reddened cheeks. Her mouth was a coral bow above a small dimpled chin.

"Lilia?" The name left his tongue of its own accord. She had been a child last he saw her. Her parents had prayed she would keep her beauty and marry out of the slums. A foolish dream, doubtless, but a kinder one than imagining her a prostitute.

Her head cocked toward him, lips stretching to bare her teeth. "Kostanos Ïerevny. You ran away to be a whore. You've done well that way, it seems."

Taunts and name-calling had long since lost their sting for him, but he flinched at the derision in her voice. "What have I done to earn that, Lilushka?"

"To me, nothing. It was Sonya you hurt with your cowardice." She looked back to Sonya, dismissing him eloquently. "Which is why you must come home, Sonyushka. You'll find no comfort in these brothels. We'll take care of you."

Sonya's hands were white on the edge of the table, her voice a slicing wire. "Like you took care of Akilina? And those children in Birthgrave?"

Lilia shrugged. "Akilina was a coward, too. And as for the children… Well, what sort of life would they have had? This city has done little enough for us—why should we care for its refuse?"

"Because we know what it's like for them. Go back to your boneyard, if that's all you're fit for. I'm done with you."

Lilia bared her teeth again, nothing like a smile. "We're your family. You'll never be done with us. As for him—" She flicked her fingers toward Gentian. "If you think he can help you, you're a fool."

Gentian and Sonya leaned forward as one, chairs scraping against the stones. But before either could reply, Lilia's spine arched, head snapping back to show the sinews of her throat. Her silent companions steadied her as her whole body stretched and curved. Her eyes rolled back in their sockets when she straightened.

"This one will be your undoing, Sonya Ïerevny." Her voice was a whispered hiss, like wind through dry grass, rat's feet over bones; all the color drained from her face. "Cleave to him and you'll end in blood and pain and darkness. Come with us, and we'll make you strong." Blood pooled in her eyes, glittering like garnets on her lashes, stark against her chalky pallor. "Stay with the whores and die."

Lilia slumped as the vision left her, swaying against her companions. Gentian's mouth was dry, his pulse sharp in his throat; he couldn't draw a breath. Beneath the table, Sonya's icy hand caught his.

"Gentian is my family," she said, low and steady. "Go home, or I'll call for the guards and their torches."

Lilia's laugh was thick and wet and filmed with red. "You're braver than that, Sonyushka. I'll see you again." She turned, and her friends turned with her.

A step fell behind them—a teashop patron stood in the doorway, staring after Lilia in shock. Gentian exhaled in a rush. He turned his next breath into a laugh, and grinned at the man. "Actors," he said, rolling his eyes.

His grip on Sonya's hand ground bone to bone.

❦

"Tell me everything," he said when they were safe in the warmth of his room. He'd checked the mirror three times, and hung every charm he owned in the window.

Sonya sighed, drawing her legs up beneath his threadbare spare blanket. "It was after my mother died. When I visited her grave I felt something in Veilgarden. A spirit. We ward against them, but this one seemed harmless. It reminded me of the veštimi. Lilia felt it too, and Akilina. We all have dead buried there.

"The spirits, the kostovi"—*bone things*, it meant in Rosian— "had lain quiet in Veilgarden for decades, long before the refugees settled there. They were small, and feared the priests with salt and silver. But when we began burying our dead around them, they stirred. They said we might help one another, like we had with the veštimi at home. Their sight in exchange for our flesh. Temporarily, of course."

Gentian turned away from the window and the darkness pressing against the warped glass. That lamp and brazier seemed tiny things against the weight of winter. He'd sent the roses to be dried, but their funereal scent lingered.

"The vigils and exorcists wouldn't bother to learn the difference," he said. Demons, the Selafaïns called any melding of flesh and spirit. Witches could deal with ghosts and spirits, but possession was anathema. The priests of Erishal and the sorcerers of the Arcanost dealt harshly with any who invited it.

"No," Sonya agreed. "I refused at first, though I couldn't stay away from the cemetery. Then women started disappearing, and everyone was afraid to walk at night. The kostovi spoke of demons stalking Oldtown and swore they could protect us. Lilia was determined to go through with it, but I stopped her. I was older, and had the most experience with the veštimi at home." She laughed harshly. "I told myself it was to protect her, but in truth

I couldn't stand the thought of someone else taking what I had wanted so much."

"What happened?" Gentian asked after she fell silent too long. The bitterness in her voice unnerved him.

"I saw. Wonderful things, terrible things. All the little spirits hiding on the rooftops and below the streets, the ancient ghosts weeping amongst the trees, faded thin as old gauze. And as they promised, I saw the demon with the knife. Or felt her, maybe—a sharp red wind sweeping through the streets. The kostovi taught me to sense her coming. I warned all that would listen, as carefully as I could. And of those who listened, none died."

"What went wrong?" Something always went wrong. The theatre had taught him that, even if he hadn't seen Lilia himself.

"At first it was hard to see. The joining, it's—" She shuddered, hugging one arm across her chest. "Like nothing I've ever known. Wild elation that leaves you spent. But the elation fades with time, and the fatigue doesn't. I watched the others grow thin and wasted—watched myself, too. And as we weakened, the kostovi grew strong. So we wanted them even more, to take their strength back.

"I saw the trap," she said, as Gentian drew breath to speak. "I've seen enough of my neighbors take comfort in laudanum to know the signs. But how could we stop when a killer stalked Little Kiva? I warned the kostovi that they took too much from us, and they promised they would control themselves." She laughed again. "I thought they meant it, before I realized we weren't the only ones they were feeding on."

Gentian swallowed. "The children in Birthgrave."

"Yes. They left Little Kiva alone, out of mockery or warped honor, but we'd made them strong enough to hunt and feed elsewhere. But I didn't know that at first. I thought it was working, that we had recreated the oracles, that we could help our people."

Her eyes glistened liquid in the lamplight. Gentian tried to speak but his tongue was thick and useless. He stared at his white-knuckled hands, and when he looked up her eyes were dry once more. "What happened?" he said at last.

"Anika died."

Anika Sirota had been Little Kiva's shining prize—a girl whose voice carried her out of the slums and into the Orpheum Tharymis, Erisín's most venerable theatre. Gentian had followed her career with equal parts hope and jealousy. Her role in *Astrophel and Satis* made her the darling of the city, until the night her golden throat was slit and her body dumped in the street. After so many other deaths ignored by the constables, that was the breaking point for Little Kiva.

"We saw the riots coming, but by then people were too angry to listen. Lilia—" She broke off, mouth twisting wryly. "I want to blame Lilia, but it was all of us. We hid in Veilgarden when the violence started, hid among the bones like cowards while our people died and houses burned."

"You couldn't have stopped it," Gentian said, crouching beside the bed and laying a hand on her ankle. The Garden had bolted its doors and shutters against the riots that swept Oldtown. Streets outside the Garden's walls were still fire-scarred, blind with broken windows. "I'm glad you're safe."

Her hand closed on his, but her stricken face didn't ease. "I was a coward. Afterward, after all that destruction and bloodshed, the kostovi were stronger than ever, and hungrier still. Akilina and I knew we had to stop them, but when she and Lilia fought, I used the distraction and fled. And brought all my troubles to your doorstep."

"You're safe here," Gentian said, using all his stagecraft to keep his voice steady and assured. "The constables and the exorcists will take care of Lilia." He almost believed it, but he remembered how scarce police and priests had been in the shantytowns.

Sonya didn't reply—he'd never been good at lying to her—but when he sat beside her and wrapped an arm over her shoulders she turned into his embrace, burying her face in the crook of his neck.

"Stay with me tonight," she whispered.

"Yes."

❦

They lay together on the narrow bed, Sonya's back curving warm against his chest. Her hair fell from its coils, teasing him with orange and rosemary. After a long, fraught silence she finally relaxed against him, burrowing into the pillows as her breath deepened.

Like any good flower, Gentian knew how to offer comfort. He ached to ease the tension in her shoulders, to kiss away the frown etched on her brow. He could be the one to give solace for once, the strong, assured one. But Lilia's prophecy echoed in his head and fear held him stiff and powerless.

A demon's trick, he tried to convince himself, a lie. But combined with Gisela's portents, he couldn't ignore it. He'd witnessed childbirth and seen fever victims vomit black blood; he imagined golden-haired Anika sprawled on the cobbles. So many ways for a woman to die in blood and pain.

Every fate can be changed, he told himself. If only he couldn't think of twenty tragedies that told him otherwise.

When Sonya began to snore, he pressed a kiss against her shoulder and closed his eyes, following her down that dark river. Dreams of her blood on his hands chased him along night's shores.

The next night the players gathered in the wings, pacing and muttering to themselves. Devi, the dark Archipelagan soprano who'd won the role of Lucretia, sang scales in the corner, while Dimitri and Yanni mimed their duel with rolled programs. Alyssum the costumer sat in a circle of lamps, cursing under her breath as she stitched stray beads and sequins back onto Lucretia's final gown. Silvia stood with her head bowed and hands clasped, reciting her cues like a prayer—Gentian hoped the saints were listening. The twins stood apart from the rest of the troupe. Gisela tuned her violin and rosined her bow; Siglinda merely watched. Gentian took care not to meet her eyes.

This was his third season with the Flores Nocturnum, and their quirks and rituals were comfortable by now. He knew better than to speak to Devi, or to take Dimitri's curses and complaints personally. His own nerves struck as they always did before the curtain rose: his mouth dried, and his bladder clenched when he reached for water. He closed his eyes and breathed through it. Worries and doubts retreated and the character stepped in to fill the void. Ilario, the seductive spirit of the mirror, who wooed poor half-mad Lucretia away from her family and her betrothed.

As he became the demon, Sonya's stories of the kostovi filled his head, settling into the spaces between his lines. He imagined himself a thing of white bone and hunger, promises and lies veined with honest desire.

At his cue, he straightened his black velvet jacket and stepped out to win his bride.

❧

Gentian returned to the shadow of the wings at intermission, sparks dancing along his nerves. From the way Devi watched him, her black eyes lambent, he knew she felt it too: this performance was more powerful than the last. The urge to pull her close and kiss her was overwhelming, though not as strong as the certainty of Elisa's wrath if he ruined both their makeup. He nearly risked it anyway, but hurried steps and Val's voice broke the tension.

He turned expecting a message from Elisa, but the stricken look on Val's face meant something worse than muffed blocking.

"What is it?" Gentian asked. His voice cracked as he set aside Ilario's hollow tones.

"It's Sonya. She's—she's gone."

"What?"

"I did as you asked—fed her and kept her occupied. We went up to the catwalks to watch the show. But halfway through the second act, something happened. She—" Val's throat worked, and one brown hand rose to his cheek, tracing the path of tears. "She ran, and now I can't find her anywhere."

Gentian's stomach cramped as if with a blow. "I know where she's gone," he whispered. It would be more than an hour till the final curtain, and longer still until he could politely extricate himself. Two hours. She would be all right for two hours....

The twins watched him from the darkness of the corridor, their faces painted masks, and he knew it for a lie.

"Find Foxglove. He'll finish the show for me."

"What?" Devi's voice rose, still humming with Lucretia's hysteria.

"It's an emergency." His throat tightened around the words. "I have to go. Fox knows the lines as well as I do."

Devi's hand closed like a manicured vise on his sleeve. "Fox can't do what you've done tonight! He's not as good to start with, and what we had out there was—" Her free hand rose, as if to snatch the word from the air. "Magic!"

She was right; even off the boards the tension still crackled between them. And she was right about Foxglove—he knew the lines as any understudy should, but the choice between him and Gentian at auditions had been no choice at all.

"What's going on?"

They both turned like guilty children at Elisa's voice. A lamp lit the stage manager's mane of bronze-dark hair into a halo, and cast her face in ominous shadow.

"Gentian is trying to leave!" Devi wailed, before he could manage a reply.

"*What?*" Her voice was a whip-crack, and Gentian flinched under the lash.

"It's an emergency," he said again. He swallowed and rallied his strength. "It's family. I'm sorry, Elisa, but I have to go. Fox can finish the show for me."

Elisa's mouth opened and snapped shut again; Valerian had returned, with the nervous Foxglove in tow. However angry she might be, she wouldn't insult a player before sending him out. She wouldn't make wild threats, either, but he read a dozen in her narrowed eyes.

"I'm sorry," he said again, shrugging out of the demon's jacket and pressing it into Foxglove's slack hands. "I'll be back as soon as I can."

He turned his back on Devi's shriek and fled. At the end of the corridor he realized he was pursued—he braced to hear Elisa telling him not to come back at all, but instead Val's hand caught his arm.

"I'm coming with you." He raised a hand before Gentian could argue. "If you think Elisa's angry now, imagine her state if you get yourself killed. Or lose your voice."

Gratitude weakened his knees. Or maybe that was only fear. "Let's go, then."

"You'll need these." The twins stepped out of the hall, pale as ghosts in the gloom. Gisela's fiddle case was slung over her shoulder; Siglinda held out two sheathed swords. Delicate, decorative things with elaborate caged hilts and scabbards glittering with paste gems. Gentian recognized them from the prop room: their blades were slender but unblunted. "It's not safe out there. And it's cold—we'll need coats."

The Veilgarden was a dark tangle between Harrowgate and the slum that had become Little Kiva, walled with stone and iron. Once it had held only trees and a few ancient tombs, their occupants long forgotten. The city, in a rare act of benevolence, had given it to the Rosians so they might bury their dead in their own ways. That grant happened long before the Ierevny family had settled here, but Gentian remembered how few graves it held when they arrived, and how many by the time he left for the Garden.

One of them belonged to his mother, another to his aunt, and he'd brought no offerings. He thought of all the flowers wilting in his room and shame stung his cheeks.

"Here?" Val asked as the carriage rattled away. He blew on his hands and shoved them deep in his pockets. Snow drifted from the low ashen sky, fat flakes that melted against streets and rooftops.

"Here." Certainty filled his stomach like ice water. And he hoped the twins would tell him if he were wrong.

Gentian checked the strange weight of the sword at his hip and started for the entrance. The scabbard clattered against the iron gate, but the snow muffled the sound. Branches creaked and scraped in the wind and snow spun around him, a hundred ghosts in the corner of his eye.

"They're not real," one of the twins said when he flinched away from a white shape in the darkness. "Mostly."

He nearly missed Sonya through the flying snow. She knelt a few yards inside the gate, her hair falling to veil the pallor of her face. She started when he called her name, flinching at his outstretched hand; he still wore Ilario's painted face. He flinched in turn from the crust of blood on her cheeks. She felt insubstantial when he helped her up, less real than the girl who'd fallen asleep in his arms the night before. They stood on a grave, he realized with a shudder.

"Come on," he said, steering her back the way they came. "You'll freeze out here."

"No!" She pulled away, strong despite her trembling limbs. "More people will die before the constables intervene, you know that. I helped start this—I have to finish it."

He wanted to argue, wanted to lie, anything to win her free of this madness. Wanted to turn on his heel and save himself. But he couldn't run from the dead any longer.

"Not alone."

"Kostya—"

"Lead the way," he said, taking her hand. "The sooner this is done, the sooner we can get out of the cold."

She glanced at the others. Val nodded, shivering miserably. "Gen's right. Let's go." The twins flanked him in silent assent, tall and pale as swan sisters.

The snow fell faster, thick enough to stick. It rimed the cracked stones of the path and limned the grave markers with luminous white. Though Veilgarden was only a small park, they couldn't see its walls, nor any lights from the city—only black-bone trees and row after row of graves. Shadows writhed and whispered around them, but Gentian kept his spine straight and reminded himself that it was only stage tricks.

Until a white hand shot out of the dark and struck his face. He shouted and stumbled, landing hard on one knee. Blood scalded his cheek and soaked his collar. When he touched the burning talon-wounds, his hand came away dripping black.

"You said it wasn't real!" He regretted speaking as the movement stretched torn skin.

"I said *mostly*," Siglinda corrected.

As Sonya pressed a scarf to Gentian's face, Gisela unslung her fiddle and opened the case. "At least it isn't raining," she muttered as she checked the strings.

At the first long note the shadows seethed even thicker, closing around the five of them. Gentian held his breath and Sonya's hand as the darkness pressed down. Then the slow, mournful opening of a toccata picked up speed. Gisela's bow flashed in the snowlight and the shadows broke and fell away. Even the snow seemed to blow away from them under the force of the music.

"Go," Siglinda said. "She can't play forever."

Gentian swallowed the taste of pain and nerves and took the bloodstained scarf from Sonya. "I'm fine," he promised. The cold helped, at least.

They moved faster with the kostovi's tricks held at bay. The night was natural once more, the graveyard smaller. The paved path ended at a thick tangle of trees. A light glowed beyond the swaying branches, warm and welcoming. He knew it for a lie.

Gisela's toccata ended and she began a trill, her hands white blurs on the strings and bow. Witch or not, the cold must pain her. Twigs poked them as they stepped into the thicket, snagged hair and clothes, but the music kept the sharp white hands away.

The light came from a mausoleum, its walls cracked and moss-veined. Costly stained glass had once filled the narrow windows;

now they gaped like sharp-toothed mouths. The heavy stone door stood ajar.

Sonya hauled the door open, tendons standing taut in her hands and wrists. Her face was a blood-streaked mask.

Lilia waited inside, crosslegged on a crumbling sarcophagus. One of her companions stood behind her, while the other curled in the corner, wrapped in moth-eaten blankets. He shook with fever, or perhaps some demon ague. Blankets and spare clothes and empty bottles littered the corners, piled next to grinning skulls and displaced corpses. Gentian's stomach roiled, but he made himself look: if he survived tonight, he had to describe it for Elisa.

Gisela's trill faltered and silence filled the room.

"I knew you'd come back," Lilia said to Sonya, "but I didn't imagine you'd bring so many guests. I don't have enough wine." The inside of the tomb was hardly warmer than the night without, but Lilia wore only a blouse and thin skirts. The gaping collar showed the starkness of her clavicles, the grooves of her sternum. Her eyes glittered with febrile light and her face was streaked with blood.

"We have to stop this, Lilia." Sonya's velvet-clad shoulders drooped with fatigue, but she pulled herself straight again. "We did what we meant to—we protected our families. But now the monster is gone and the kostovi have grown too strong and too hungry."

Lilia laughed, sharp and piercing as a violin. "There will always be new monsters. And we both know about hunger, don't we?" She rose from her seat with a weightless marionette grace. "I'm not hungry anymore, Sonyushka, and you don't have to be either."

"I would rather starve than kill children and tired grandmothers."

Lilia's hand looked fragile as a doll's, but Sonya rocked from the force of the blow. Gentian coiled to intervene, but Siglinda's grip on his sleeve held him. The four actors huddled in the corner, giving the two women room. They had become extras in this tableau. Witnesses.

Sonya straightened, lifting her chin. A drop of blood glittered at the corner of her mouth. In the face of her composure, Lilia turned away and spat.

"Damn you and your sanctimony. Always so noble. As if you weren't the same refugee trash as the rest of us. Kostya knew better than to tie himself to you. I should have known, too."

Gentian's scabbing jaw clenched with the effort to stay quiet. Sonya didn't so much as glance at him.

"It isn't me you've tied yourself to," she said quietly.

"Of course it is. You're everyone's favorite—Grandmother's, Akilina's, Symon's." At the last she spun to kick a pebble at the man curled in the corner. He didn't stir as it bounced off him. "And now you're their favorite too." She raised her hands to encompass the shadowed ceiling. When Gentian looked, he saw pale shapes hovering there, white and translucent as misted breath. "I would suck your bones dry to be rid of your harping, but they won't let me. Because they want you more than me."

With that, the rage drained from her like wine from a broken flask. Lilia slumped to her knees, tears of salt rinsing the ašara from her face.

Sonya's hair veiled her face, but her voice was cracked and gentle. "Oh, Lilushka." She knelt beside Lilia, one arm circling the girl's thin shoulders. "I'm sorry," she whispered. "I never meant to hurt you." Her left hand stroked Lilia's tangled hair. Her right hand was in her pocket.

Anticipation knotted painfully in Gentian's stomach. He wanted to cry out, to stop what he knew was coming, but he was speechless as poor mute Thracian.

"I just wanted— I just wanted—" Lilia's want was lost as she broke into wet hiccupping sobs on Sonya's shoulder, but Gentian could imagine it easily. Warmth. Safety. Companionship without guilt. All the things he'd wanted when he turned his back on his family.

"It's all right," Sonya said. "Forgive me."

She drew her hand from her pocket and the tiny silver knife glittered in the lamplight. With one motion, she yanked Lilia's head back and sank the blade into her straining throat. Blood spurted as she twisted.

Lilia let out a terrible gasp, crimson bubbles bursting on her lips. Her back arched, and red streaked her golden hair as her heels carved ruts in the packed earth. Sonya stumbled back, her bloody hand pressed to her mouth.

They might have stood in petrified silence till Lilia stopped kicking, but the man behind the bier—so quiet Gentian had forgotten he wasn't furniture—screamed and leapt at Sonya, tripping over the sarcophagus. Her silver knife was still in Lilia's throat.

It was Val who moved while Gentian was frozen. With the grace of a dozen staged duels, he drew his blade and lunged. The sword flashed and the man's shout ended in a liquid gurgle and hot spray. The tomb, which had smelled of dust and stone and winter, stank like an abattoir.

The kostovi had made no move to save their followers. Now they drifted down from the ceiling like fog, curling greedily against the blood that soaked the earth.

"It's over," Val whispered. His dark face had drained the color of milky tea, but the blade in his hand didn't tremble.

"No," Siglinda said. "These poor fools might be dead, but the spirits are fat and healthy. They'll find fresh meat to serve them. And you know they won't leave you in peace." That last she spoke to Sonya, who nodded.

"I know." Her voice was low and rough, scraped hollow. Her laugh sounded even worse. "Lilia was right—they always did like me best."

"You know what you have to do," said Gisela, cradling her violin like a babe.

"I know," Sonya said again. She shrugged off the green velvet jacket and handed it to Siglinda. "I'm sorry about the blood, but I think it will wash out." The blouse hung loose on her thin frame and her arms roughened in the chill.

"What are you doing?" Gentian asked, forcing his tongue to move at last. His clawed cheek throbbed; his hands clenched so tightly they'd gone numb.

"I have to lay them to rest again." She gestured to the still-feeding kostovi. Their white forms were thicker now, the lines of white talons and limbs clear. Pale tongues lapped at the earth, licked Lilia's waxen face clean.

"How?"

Sonya didn't answer, staring at the cooling corpse of the girl who had been her friend. It was Siglinda who spoke into the silence.

"They need a prison, and a sacrifice to seal it. Demons can die, once they've taken flesh."

Gentian looked from the impassive twins to Sonya, something horrible hatching in his stomach. "No. No. You can't mean it. You can't—"

"Who else will? I don't want this. Please believe that I don't. But I can do it now and no one else will be hurt. I can't let anyone else suffer."

"I'll suffer." Shame stung his face as soon as he said it—selfish to the last.

"Oh, Kostya. Gentian." She drew him close and kissed his uninjured cheek. He felt the bloody print of her lips like a brand. "You'll go on. You're better at that than any of us." She raised a hand as he drew breath. "You're so beautiful on the stage. I'm proud of you. And maybe—" Her fingers trailed down his chest and fell away. "Maybe we all have something we can't live with. Something we have to run from. This is mine."

"I'll…" He choked on salt and snot. "I'll write you a play. A play for you, and for Mother, and Grandmother. For all of us. So everyone will know who we are."

Her smile was crooked and sad beneath the blood. "They'd like that. I'd like that."

Somewhere in Harrowgate, a bell tolled the hour. Back at the Rhodon, Livius would have found Lucretia by now, dead in the garden, surrounded by glittering shards of mirror. Sonya's smile vanished, replaced by grim resolve.

"I have to ask your help again," she said, taking Gentian's hand. " A sacrifice made in love is stronger still."

His eyes stung. He'd thought his mother asked too much, but this…. But five years of cowardice were more than enough. He nodded.

Sonya knelt, reaching carefully into the writhing tangle of spirits to free her knife from Lilia's throat. White hands clutched her, white tongues scraping her skin, but they let her go, turning back to the dead blood welling where the blade had been.

"Here," Sonya called, slashing her left hand. "Here's something fresher."

The kostovi flowed like smoke, coiling around her legs and rushing toward the dripping wound. She whispered to them— an invitation, an invocation. Beneath the murmur of her voice, Gisela's violin rose as well, the sweet notes of a cradle song meant to soothe and lure.

Sonya opened her mouth and the spirits filled her, stretching her throat as she swallowed them down. Her back arched as she gasped, her whole body straining like a string pulled taut. Then she snapped forward and her eyes were white and leaking blood.

"Stay with us," she said to Gentian, her voice a choral swell, her demon's face transfigured with inhuman beauty. "Fame and adoration will be yours with us beside you. Crowds will weep for you and shower you with riches. Kings will fall at your feet and you'll never be hungry again."

Her voice was black velvet and poppy wine, the shores of night itself. Her hair fell back, baring the planes and arches of her face, so like his own. Ilaria, the mirror to show his dreams. "Stay with me," she said, reaching out one long white hand. All he had to do was take it, and those dreams would come true.

Never taking his eyes from hers, Gentian drew his sword. The tip pressed beneath her left breast, denting white cloth and the flesh beneath.

"You wouldn't," the demon crooned. But that velvet voice cracked, and the unearthly light in her eyes dimmed till they were brown and human again.

"Please."

With all his weight behind the blade, Gentian stepped toward her.

By the time they sank to the ground, her blood warm on his hands and chest, she was only Sonya, and still.

Three days later, Sonya Ïerevny was laid beside her mother and her aunt, her grandmother and all their other kin who had died in Erisín. The priestess spoke the service in Rosian, if not quite as orthodox as a rite as would have been said at home.

More living than dead filled Veilgarden that day, pressed shoulder to shoulder, draped in veils the color of ashes. A few recognized Gentian, but even more stared—whether at his scabbed face or velvet coat or Val's arm around his waist he couldn't say.

Sunset rinsed the sky violet and incarnadine as the final hymn began, and the song chased the sun behind the rooftops. When the final verse faded, Gentian stepped forward to lay his armful of unseasonal flowers on the grave. No roses, but a cluster of gentians shone like blue flame amid the wildflowers. The other mourners left gifts as well—flowers and candles and trinkets, folded sheets of poetry. The wind that ruffled the petals was light and gentle, and no whispers carried through the chill air.

"Come on," Val said as the service broke up, turning Gentian away. "You need to eat."

He nodded, though his throat was tight and his stomach dead. In Little Kiva, all those who mourned Sonya would gather for dinner tonight. They would serve old family recipes and tell stories about the deceased, to send her spirit happily into the Halls of Night. A few of her neighbors might have welcomed him, but Gentian couldn't join them.

"Where are we going?" he finally asked, when he realized they weren't walking back to the Garden, but deeper into Oldtown.

"To Altarlight," Val said, threading his arm through Gentian's. "My sister wants to meet you."

The Sergeant
AND THE GENERAL

JASPER KENT

Mellé was a strange cove; a veteran of Spain and Moscow and Waterloo. He was one of the first people I met when I came to Paris from Toulouse to study medicine. I found rooms on the fourth floor of a house in the *Rue du Fer à Moulin*. The place was occupied mostly by some of the university's better off students except, so the concierge told me, for the garret, which was Mellé's home.

I saw him climbing the stairs on my first evening there, and immediately deduced that he was nothing to do with the university. I offered him a greeting, at which he grunted neutrally, but he didn't stay to exchange pleasantries. Two days later, I was having dinner in Monsieur Pavart's tavern, a few doors down, when Mellé entered. The place was crowded, and it was clear he would have to share a table, so I called over to him.

'Sergeant Mellé!'

He looked at me, and then around the room. On seeing there was no alternative he shrugged and came over to join me.

'I'll take your presence here as a recommendation,' I said.

'It's close,' he replied. 'And they don't fuss.'

Almost as soon as he had sat, a girl came over and gave him a glass of red wine. She didn't ask him if he wanted to eat. I held out the basket of bread that had come with my food and offered it to him.

'I never share food,' he said.

I put it back down. 'How long have you lived here?' I asked.

'Since Waterloo.'

I studied him. Back home I had met several veterans of the wars and whilst many were proud to speak of all their battles, some avoided the subject of the emperor's final humiliation. For my part, I was fascinated to hear their stories; I was too young to remember a time before Bonaparte.

'A close run thing, I hear,' I said, letting him choose whether to pick up the subject.

'Lost long before it began.'

From there he was easy to coax into a detailed discussion, not just of Waterloo, but of all his battles and campaigns. When we were a few minutes into it, the girl returned and put in front of him a bowl of plain rice. Before even tasting it he reached into his waistcoat pocket and produced a little paper sachet, twisted closed at the top. He opened it and poured its contents—a black powder that I suspected might be pepper—onto his rice. He made no response to my quizzical gaze, but began to eat, continuing his stories of the wars between mouthfuls. As soon as he had finished his meal, he gave me a brief *au revoir* and departed. He didn't even attempt to settle his bill, but they clearly knew him.

After that we conversed quite frequently at the tavern. He always ate the same—a bowl of rice accompanied by a glass of red wine. We also passed each other more than once on the stairs of our lodgings, but there he never stopped to chat.

It was in late November, when I was in the tavern alone, that the proprietor himself, Pavart, happened to serve me. We spoke a little, and then he said something which very much surprised me.

'You seem to be getting on well with your landlord.'

'Who?' In truth, I had no idea who my landlord was. I paid my rent to the concierge and presumed that it in turn was presented to some restored baron whose travels rarely took him close to the Left Bank.

'Sergeant Mellé,' explained Pavart.

'Mellé?' I asked. 'I'm surprised he can afford the rent on his room.'

'He doesn't have to. He owns it; bought it when the emperor went to Saint Helena.'

'Bought it with what?'

'Don't you listen to his stories? They all came back rich from Moscow—those that did come back. He paid in diamonds—at least, so I heard.'

It seemed an unlikely notion, but Pavart had no reason to lie, and the next time I spoke to Mellé I asked him about it. He offered no denial.

'But why hide away in the attic?' I pressed him. 'It must be tiny.'

'I don't need any more space. And it's far from the street. I don't like the noise.'

'Noise?'

'The noise of the horses!' he snapped.

His comment about horses meant that I was somewhat apprehensive when it came to our next conversation of any import. The winter had passed and as the summer of 1819 began to approach, I'd written to my father complaining of how little I was seeing beyond the centre of Paris. His solution—as had been my hope—was to offer to buy me a horse. I'd never heard anyone mention a stable in our building, but the other three lodging houses off the courtyard were of almost identical design, and all had stables beneath. I could even guess which door led to ours, though it was always protected by a hefty lock. I raised the issue with Mellé.

'I presume you have stables beneath the house.'

'What of it?' he replied.

'I was thinking of getting a horse. Obviously it would be convenient if...'

'No!' he snapped, before I could finish. Then he calmed a little. 'It's a mess down there. Not good enough for a horse.'

'That could be fixed,' I protested.

'Too expensive,' he muttered.

Our meal ended quickly and in silence.

After that, the idea of my getting a horse didn't make much progress. It would have been easy enough for me to find stabling nearby, but that would have required more effort than I was prepared to give. It wasn't long though before I got to see the house's stables for myself. It began when I encountered another old soldier coming down the stairs from what I could only presume was an attempt to visit Mellé, whom I'd seen leave the house earlier.

'Were you looking for Sergeant Mellé?' I asked him.

'He's not there,' said the man gruffly.

'Should I tell him who called?'

The man's face twisted into a nasty half smile. 'Tell him Corporal Dumont paid him a visit,' he said.

I never got a chance to speak to Mellé about it. The following day, when I was returning home from my studies, I saw Dumont leaving the house again. Since I'd last encountered him, his face had acquired a new and distinguishing feature: a livid bruise to his right eye that looked quite fresh. He glanced from side to side and then crossed the courtyard and exited into the street. On some instinct I waited, stepping back into the shadows. Sure enough, just moments later, Mellé emerged too, carrying a lantern. He didn't make for the street, but turned sharply left and went to the door that I presumed led down to the stable. He unfastened the heavy iron padlock and went inside. I waited a moment longer, then scampered across to see what lay within.

From the door, a long slope led down beneath the building, shallow enough for a horse to walk down without losing its footing. It was a typical design for Paris. Out in Toulouse we had space enough to put our stables beside our houses, but here in the capital they'd been building one beneath the other for centuries. I took a few paces forward. On one side of the ramp was a solid wall, but on the left there was no barrier. Below me, the floor of the stable was covered with fresh straw. Beyond that, along the far wall, stood the stalls for individual horses—five of them in total. The light of Mellé's lantern shone out of the second from the left.

I crept down the slope and then doubled back to that stall. The gate was open. Inside, I saw only the lantern, hanging from a hook on the wall. Of the sergeant there was no sign.

'That's Harpagon,' said a voice from behind me, which I knew at once to belong to Mellé.

'Harpagon?' I asked, turning to see him slumped in the corner, almost directly beneath the top of the ramp.

'He took me all the way to Moscow; and some of the way back. They got him at Krasnoi.'

'Got him?'

'The Russians. Shot him from under me. He's a fine creature though don't you think?'

I was confounded for what to say, but a simple 'Yes,' seemed to satisfy him. He rose and walked over into the stall, gazing slightly upwards, as though at the head of the horse that had once stood there. He picked up the lantern and walked away. I followed. He passed the middle of the five stalls and headed on to the fourth.

'They don't get on, you see,' he muttered, 'so it's best to keep a distance between them.'

He unbolted the gate of the stall and opened it, holding his lantern high to illuminate what was within.

'And this,' he announced proudly, 'is the General.' Again, the space was empty, but for some straw on the ground, and oats in the trough. 'He got me as far as... He got me home.' The pause in the middle of Mellé's words was barely perceptible. Again he stared forwards, with his head slightly inclined. My guess would be that the General was somewhat taller than Harpagon, but to think like that, I realized, was to rely upon the imaginings of a madman.

As the lantern swung from side to side in his frail hand, I saw that the stall was in fact, not quite empty. In the straw, close to the back wall, something glinted. I stepped forward to examine it more closely. I could only suppose that I was walking through the very space where Mellé believed the creature to be standing, but he did not object.

There in the hay was what had caught my eye: it was made of silver—a brooch in the shape of a horse, small enough to fit into the palm of my hand. I made to pick it up.

'Don't!' said Mellé quietly from behind me. 'He's nervous with strangers.'

I withdrew my hand, and looked more closely. It was unremarkable, somewhat battered in fact. It looked as though there had once been a jewel to mark its eye.

'We must go now,' said the sergeant.

I nodded, but spent a few more moments looking at the silver horse that was the stable's only occupant. Then I stood, glancing around the stall. Finally I turned to Mellé, ready to leave. I was alone. He had hung the lamp from the wall, but of him there was no sign. I dashed out of the stall, just in time to see his feet at the top of the ramp, exiting into the courtyard. I realized in an instant that I was trapped. There was no other exit than the one he had just taken, and I remembered the heavy padlock.

I raced up the slope, but when I reached the top, he had made no attempt to close the door. He stood quietly in the twilight, gazing upwards towards the gap of sky, circled by the tall buildings that surrounded us.

I began to close the door, but he put his hand on my arm to stop me.

'Time to set them free, don't you think?' he said. I could make no reply. I stood there for a few moments, uncomfortable and out of place. 'Best that you leave us,' he added. I needed no second bidding, but went to my rooms. When I looked back down into the courtyard, he was gone.

I never properly spoke to Sergeant Mellé again. I saw him, briefly, the following day. I'd just turned into the street and he was about half way down. Apart from us, it was empty, but Mellé didn't appear to find it so. It was as though he were being buffeted from all sides—pushed by a crowd. He could have been mistaken for a drunk, but his movements were not of his own volition. They were sudden and sharp, as if something very big and very strong had run into him. He had his arms up to protect him and I realized that they were too high for it to have been a crowd of people who assailed him. It was easy enough for me to guess what it was—or what he thought it was.

He'd managed to make his way to the door of our building, but still he struggled to get any further. He shouted a single word, '*Pojalsta!*' and then broke free and made it in through the door. When I got level with the house myself, there were no signs of anything untoward; nor had I expected there to be any.

That night, however, was the most terrifying of my life. It was well into the small hours, and I'd been asleep for some time when I suddenly awoke. There had been no sound to disturb me, but I felt the undeniable sense that someone was outside my room. I went to the door and opened it. The landing and stairs beyond were empty, dimly illuminated by the candles that the concierge lit every night before retiring. It was a broad staircase, ascending in a square spiral as it clung to three of the walls of the stairwell and level on the fourth to allow access to the apartments. Leaning over the banister, one could see down to the hallway on the ground floor, or right up to the rafters amongst which Mellé's rooms nestled.

Then I heard it; the sound of hooves walking slowly on a hard surface—hard just like the stone staircase. I could hear them circling; not around me, but around the stairs, coming closer and then further away, but on each circuit, rising another storey. I looked over the balustrade, but could see only the empty steps of the floor directly below me. I stepped back into the doorway of my rooms, and at that moment, the hoof falls broke into a gallop.

A sudden panic took me, and I dove into the safety of my apartment, slamming the door shut behind me and standing, panting, with my back to it. I heard the horse—I felt sure from the sound there was only one of them—running past and then continuing up the stairs towards the garret. Then it stopped and whinnied, and I heard the sound of iron shoes scraping against a wooden door. Then—silence.

The following morning, I went up and knocked on Mellé's door, but there was no reply. In the evening, I did the same, with identical reward. That night I couldn't sleep and so when the sound first came I was able to look at my watch. It was a little before three. This time I stayed in bed, but I could hear the sounds as clearly as if I'd gone outside. Tonight there was no hesitation. The horse began at a trot, and accelerated to a gallop, its hooves now confident on the familiar surface beneath them. It dashed past my rooms and upwards to pound on Mellé's door. Again silence followed.

That morning, my knocks at the sergeant's door still received no answer but in the evening, he at last responded, however unhelpfully.

'Go to Hell!'

'Are you all right?' I persisted.

'You heard me.'

'Sergeant Mellé!'

There was no further answer. I knocked again and then tried the door, but it was locked. He had told me to leave and it was his house. I could hardly break in. I asked my neighbours, but they had heard nothing during the night. Only a few of them had ever exchanged more than a 'Good day' with him.

On the third night I knew that I would have to stand my ground. Again I did not sleep, and despite my exhaustion from the previous night, I felt no real desire to. The sound began at just the same hour, and I immediately went out of my rooms and onto the landing. Tonight the hooves truly thundered. The beast must have been huge, and bounded up the stairs at a pace that I could hardly conceive.

Soon I knew that it was on the floor immediately below mine, and I peered into the gloom of the stairwell to catch a glimpse of it. The volume was greater than ever, but still there was no hint of it in the shadows. Now it was coming up the last flight, taking the whole of it in perhaps three bounds, and yet still it did not reveal itself to my eyes. I felt the whoosh of air as it passed, smelt its odour and heard its breathing—but I saw nothing.

In a moment it was past me, across the flat landing and onto the next flight. I rushed in pursuit—if one can pursue a creature that one cannot see—but it quickly drew away from me. I was only on the fifth floor when I once again heard its hooves scraping—knocking, almost—on Mellé's door, begging to be let in.

But tonight I heard a new sound: the rattle of a latch, followed by the squeak of hinges. The door was opening. As I reached the very top of the stairs, my head almost at the point of the roof, I looked along the short corridor and saw that Mellé's door was open. The sergeant himself was standing there holding it, as if inviting someone in. As I approached, our eyes met. His face was calm—resigned. In a moment he turned away, closing the door behind him. I ran to it and tried to open in, but it was already locked. I hammered my fists against it and called his name, but there was no reply. Eventually a voice shouted from below.

'Keep it down, will you? People are trying to sleep.'

I stopped, and all was silent. I stood there for several minutes, but in the end I knew that there was nothing I could do. I went back down to my room.

The following day, again, I knocked on Mellé's door, both in the morning and the evening, but there was no response. That night, I determined, I would not follow the creature up to the sergeant's room, but precede it. I'd be there ready when it arrived and if Mellé chose to open his door then I would grab him and force him to explain to me what was going on. But with so little sleep over the previous days, I dozed off. I slept until morning. If the horse had come that night, it had not awoken me. But I knew just what a noise it made, and felt sure that it had not come.

Again there was no response when I knocked at the door. I asked the concierge if he had seen anything, but the answer was a shake of the head, and a concerned look. That night I did manage to keep awake, and the horse most certainly did not pass by.

When I got back from the university the following day, I didn't even attempt to speak to the sergeant; a different idea had occurred to me. I went straight to my rooms to fetch a candle, then back down to the courtyard and over to the stable door. It was still unlocked. I went in and descended the ramp. Nothing had changed since my visit with Mellé. The straw was still strewn on the floor; the gates of the two stalls we had visited remained open.

I went straight to the nearer of them. The lantern he had left there still hung from the wall, long since burned out. My candle offered a far dimmer light, but it was enough for me to see that the little silver brooch was missing. I knelt down, placing my light carefully away from the straw, and began to search through, but there was nothing. The silver horse was gone.

When I stepped back into the courtyard, they were just bringing Mellé's body out of the house. There was a sheet covering his face, but I had no doubt as to who it was. The concierge's wife stood near the gate, looking tearful. I went up and spoke to her.

'We were worried,' she said. 'He could be a bit of a misery, but he never shut himself away for that long. We had to break the door down—and that's when we found him. He was cold as stone; must have been dead for days.'

I walked over to the two men who were carrying him. 'May I look?' I asked. 'I'm a doctor.' It was an exaggeration, but they glanced over at the concierge, who had followed them out of the house, and he nodded, not seeming to know the difference between a student and a true practitioner. I drew back the sheet and looked at Mellé. Though he was dead, he expressed the same look of calm acceptance that I had briefly seen as he closed the door to his room two nights before. Only one wound marred his face. It was obviously the cause of his death, but few other than me would accept it for what it was.

It was an arc, almost a semicircle, imprinted as a bloody mark on his forehead. If I had taken my forefinger and thumb and bent them appropriately, I could have produced an almost exact match in size and shape. It was clear that the blow had cracked his skull; even the most qualified doctor would have agreed with me on that. Death would have been very quick. Where most doctors and I would differ would be over the matter of what had caused the blow itself. But over those doctors, I had two advantages. Firstly, I knew what had visited him the night he died and secondly, I had seen such an injury before.

It had been in Toulouse, when I was about fourteen. A farm-hand had been drunk, and when his horse refused to pull the plough, he had beaten it. The horse kicked back, kicked the man in the dead centre of his skull, killing him in a second, and leaving just that same mark. The only difference was that horse in Toulouse had been real.

I covered his face again and his bearers began to move on. As they did, his arm dropped down on one side. I knelt down to tuck it back, but in doing so, I felt something hard and cold grasped in his hand. I slipped it unnoticed into mine.

That night, when everything was quiet, I returned the little silver horse to its proper place in the stables. God knew what would become of it when the house was sold, but I felt I had done my duty. Before I put it there, I'd had a chance to examine it more closely. Just as I'd thought, there had once been some kind of gem to represent the eye, but it was no more. It was the reverse side that interested me most. Into the soft silver, a name had been scratched—I say scratched rather than engraved, for it was an amateur job. I could only suppose Mellé had done it himself. The name was familiar to me, and would have been even more so to any veteran of Moscow. And it chimed with the way Mellé had described the horse in whose stall I now stood. It was the name of the man who had defeated all of France in 1812 and also, I guessed, the name not of a man, but of a creature who had been just as successful in defeating a single French sergeant.

The inscription read: 'General Kutuzov.'

⚜

General Kutuzov saved my life; for a while, at least. I remember the first time I saw him. He was difficult to make out, being white, and white being the predominant colour of the landscape to the west of the Berezina at that time of year, but the usual blizzard had subsided a little and I was just able to catch sight of him. He was bending down, nibbling at the ground in a way that indicated either he had gone crazy with hunger or, by some miracle, had managed to clear away a patch of snow and uncover some small tuft of grass beneath.

I should explain that this wasn't *the* General Kutuzov, the field marshal of Alexander's armies, who had routed us from Moscow and sent us on this long, cold, desperate march back across Europe in search of safety. The General Kutuzov that I saw burying his nose in the snow as I stumbled through the fields, hungry and alone, wondering whether it would be the cold or starvation or a Russian bullet that did for me in the end, was a horse.

My own horse, Harpagon, had been shot from under me at Krasnoi—died in a second, thank God, and from then on I'd been on foot. I knew what they'd do to Harpagon. We were at the head of the troops and got the best of the spoils from each village and town we came to. In the refor, they had to take what we left behind. And if we left behind a dead horse, so much the better. I reckoned they could have marched faster, but chose not to—they hung just behind the artillery, waiting until a horse became too weak to pull its gun. Then it would be left behind—and the gun too, but that wasn't what they were interested in. That was foot soldiers for you. A dragoon would never think of it.

I went over to him, saying a few encouraging words in French, though at first I had no idea which nation's army he belonged to. I approached him from his left—that's the way my father had always taught me to with a strange horse, back on the farm in Condé, though everyone else I ever spoke to about it said it was a myth. But it had worked for me for thirty-four years, and I wasn't going to change now. He was a little nervous, but as soon as I'd got his reins and patted his neck, he turned his head towards me and seemed to accept me. I felt his lips and tongue on my fingers, searching for some little treat that he'd clearly been accustomed to and which I did not have, but even without, the action helped us to become friends.

Then I carried out a general inspection, starting with his hooves. He'd been shod recently, and not by a French smithy; I could tell that for sure. Each shoe had three little calkins on it—nothing huge, but enough to dig into compacted snow on the road and gain a little extra grip. I'd seen too many French horses sliding on the icy surfaces, eventually to fall with legs splayed out at an angle that the Almighty could never have intended. And once they were down, it was almost impossible to get them up again, not with your own feet slipping as badly as theirs and with your brothers in arms rushing past to find somewhere warm to spend the night. You'd have thought that we'd have learned a few Russian tricks, but in truth we didn't have time. When we'd arrived in Moscow, in August, it had been miserably hot. We hadn't really been prepared for weather like that, but at least we understood it better than this.

All four shoes were in excellent condition, as was his physique in general. He was hungry, to be sure—you could tell that by the way he kept snuffling around in the snow—but it was only to the extent of an empty belly and a shortage of fat. It hadn't got to his muscle yet; that was the important thing. It was only when I'd circled almost all the way around that I saw his one blemish; he was missing his right eye. I couldn't make out precisely what had caused it, but it was a recent wound—not enough to justify his rider abandoning him, but perhaps whatever assault had caused this injury to the horse had proved fatal to his master. There was no sign of a body, but the unrelenting snow covered things quickly round here.

Whatever its cause, his missing eye did nothing to prevent me from thanking God for providing him as the means of my deliverance. It even inspired me to come up with his name; he was Russian and he possessed only one eye—what else could I choose but General Kutuzov?

I went back round to his left side. '*Ya tebya loobloo*,' I said. I love you. It was one of the few Russian phrases I knew, and though whenever I'd used it in the past it had raised a smile, it had never reduced the fee I was charged. I don't imagine General Kutuzov understood it any more than he would have done if I'd spoken French. His single eye glanced back and forth across me. I opened my knapsack and reached inside, bringing out a parcel. Kutuzov caught the scent and turned his head excitedly. I got out my little saucepan as well—it was the closest thing I had to a bowl. I'd left Harpagon's nosebag with him where he lay.

I poured some of the oatmeal into the pan and put it under Kutuzov's nose. He lowered his head and devoured it in seconds, pushing the pan away from him and following it as his tongue delved into every corner, trying to gain the last morsel of sustenance. He was hungrier than I was. I gave him a little more of the oatmeal. I could have used it to make some cakes for myself, but I made a decision that henceforth it was to be his, not mine. I had some rice and a little flour, which were more use to me.

And then there were those six boiled potatoes that I'd found in a pot on a dead fire. The man who'd been cooking them—

a Bavarian I guessed from his shako—was dead too. He'd fallen asleep and his fire had gone out and he had frozen. I took his potatoes, smashing the ice that encased them.

As he was eating, I threw my saddlebag over Kutuzov's hips. I'd been carrying it on my shoulder since Harpagon had fallen. Watching Kutuzov eat made me hungry. I'd been rationing myself carefully, but finding the horse changed all that. The journey now would be quicker, so I could eat more frequently. I reached into my knapsack and pulled out one of the potatoes. It was frozen—hard as stone. I tried to bite it, but the best I could do was to scrape away a few slivers with my front teeth, eating like a rat. I dug my way under my great coat, through three layers of shirts, and eventually found the pocket of my breeches and slipped the potato in there. It was not so close to my flesh as to freeze me, but in an hour or so it might warm up enough to be edible.

I led General Kutuzov out to the path that ran alongside the field, where I checked his saddle. I tightened the cinch and then mounted. He whinnied and sidestepped a few paces, but didn't seem too discomforted. I drove my heels into his side and Kutuzov walked forward. I could ask no more of him. He seemed tempted to trot, but I held him back. It was not speed of travel that I sought from him, but certainty. And rest. If Kutuzov could be my Saint Christopher then the strength I conserved could prove enough to make the difference between my return to France and frozen death in this godforsaken wilderness.

We walked on until nightfall, and then for a while longer, until it was almost too dark for me to see the path in front of us. I didn't even really know where we were going, more than heading vaguely west. Vilna would be the next big town, and if I could get there, I'd be able to rejoin the main body of the army. There had been talk that we might even make a stand, reinforced by the troops that the emperor had left in the city, and per-haps by the locals, who hated the Russians even more than we did. It was getting colder though, as if that were possible, and I kept going in the hope of finding some shelter. At last, through the gloom, I saw something. It wasn't much—just an old shed, with one of its wooden walls almost completely broken in. But it would be enough, as long as the wind continued to blow at us from the other side.

I dismounted and led Kutuzov in. There was no straw, not even under the mounds of drifted snow that I poked at with my bayonet. The horse gave me a mournful look with his one eye and I knew what he wanted. I poured a little more of the oat-meal into my saucepan, and he ate it as greedily as before. Then I remembered my potato. I reached through the layers of clothing and found my pocket again. I'd left it there too long and with the motion of my riding it had been reduced to a mush. But I wasn't going to waste it. I pulled out a handful of the pale, yellow paste and examined it. It was grubby with dirt from my clothes, and I could see a couple of lice mixed in there too. It didn't put me off from shovelling it down my throat, and going back until I'd scraped out every last little bit I could find. The lice had been devouring me for long enough; I wasn't going to get picky when it came to consuming them.

I pulled away some of the wood that was left in the broken down wall and snapped the shards into smaller pieces to make a fire. Then I went outside. In an instant I could feel how much protection even that humble shelter gave us from the weather. The wind was up again and although there was no new snow, what lay on the ground was being picked up and blasted through the air with enough force to make you think it was cutting through your cheek. I stayed just long enough to strip a few dead twigs off the nearest tree to use as kindling, then went back inside.

Kutuzov was already asleep. His eye was closed and his right rear leg was bent slightly, so that it just rested on the tip of its hoof. The other three legs were locked and steady. I lit the fire by igniting a little gunpowder in the pan of my musket, which in turn lit the kindling. My dinner was plain rice, boiled in melted snow. I hadn't tasted meat since Orsha, but I wasn't obsessed by it like most of them were.

It was still dark when I awoke, just like it was for sixteen hours of the day out here in December. I didn't know what had roused me, but I immediately sensed that General Kutuzov was uneasy. The fire was out and it was too dark for me to look at my pocket watch. Then I heard voices. They came from behind the back wall of the shed, against which Kutuzov was standing. I didn't fancy trying to squeeze behind him, nervous as he was, so instead I mounted him, and leaned over to peep through a gap in the rough wooden slats.

Cossacks. There was no doubt about it—around thirty of them. Since we left Moscow it had been them that had caused us the most trouble. Against a regular army, there was always some hope that we could entrench and make a stand, but the Cossacks swarmed around us like flies, never enough of them to seriously do battle with, but sufficient to pick off any stragglers and stop us being ready for the main body of the army when it arrived.

There were two options. We could stay there, keeping quiet, and hope the squad went on its way, or we could make a dash for it. The idea that that they wouldn't even bother to look inside the shed was pretty remote. Kutuzov's agitation hinted at his instinct to leave, and I agreed with him. I gathered my musket and knapsack and then we were off, heading directly away from them, keeping the building in which we'd spent the night between us for as long as possible before they could spot us. They might have heard, but that was a necessary risk. We went at full gallop, putting as much distance between us and them as we could.

I'd guessed, but I'd never known, what a truly fine creature General Kutuzov was. On the path, we'd never gone faster than a trot—a packhorse could have done as well—but now as we galloped across the open, snowy fields, I felt a rush of speed that I had rarely known before; never on the farm, and even with Harpagon, only briefly when we charged into battle. With Kutuzov, it was not merely his speed, but his stamina that made him such a wonderful beast. Even if a few of the Cossacks could match his pace, none would maintain it.

The fields were bounded mostly by hedgerows, which Kutuzov needed only a little encouragement to leap over. The fifth of these was preceded by a shallow ditch, making the hurdle even longer, but he took it comfortably in his stride, despite the darkness. There was light in the sky in the east now, which was scarcely enough for me to see by, but somehow Kutuzov seemed almost to smell the obstacles in his way. I chanced a look behind us and saw that the Cossacks had indeed spotted of us, and a group of eight or ten had set off in pursuit, but already they were beginning to give up. We carried on across three more fields, but by then I could tell that the horse was tiring. I pulled him up and we continued at a trot which soon became a walk. I patted his neck and then leaned forwards to kiss it. Then another word of Russian came back to me.

'*Spasiba,*' I said. It was the first occasion I'd had to thank any Russian since the campaign began. I turned right, so that the rising sun was behind us. There was another hedge and then a fence for us to negotiate, and whereas once I would have looked up and down them for a suitable gap, now I knew that I could gee Kutuzov up to a short burst of speed, and together we would sail over the obstacle. Beyond the fence we found a pathway. I don't think it was the one we'd been on before, but it ran in roughly the same direction. We had to hit some kind of road eventually.

It was after a couple of hours that we encountered the Cossacks again. I think it was the same ones—they must have guessed the direction we'd be heading. There were only two of them now. I don't suppose it needed more to deal with a lone rider, but they didn't guess the calibre of the creature I had under me. The path was just entering a small stretch of woodland, and they came at us from the side. I dug my heels firmly into Kutuzov's flank and he was off.

The path through the wood was reasonably clear, but still it was too risky to go on at a full gallop. I turned and was horrified to see how close the two Cossacks were to us. My musket was useless from the back of a horse, but my pistol was loaded. I drew it and slowed Kutuzov fractionally as I aimed and squeezed the trigger. I felt no certainty that the powder would still be in a state to burn, but I was pleased to see the flash of its explosion, and even more so to see one of the two men fall from his horse. His comrade didn't stop to look. I turned forward again and urged the General onwards once more, knowing that our lone pursuer would undoubtedly return fire. I heard the report of his gun, but the bullet was wide, injuring neither me nor Kutuzov.

We raced on. A glance over my shoulder showed me that the sole Cossack had not given up his chase, but inevitably he was falling back. Suddenly I felt a lurch and Kutuzov rose into the air, taking me with him. A tree had been lying across the path in front of us, covered in snow. I might not have seen it even if I'd been looking, but the horse had taken it easily in his stride. I refocused my attention on the road. Some way on, just in the trees, I noticed movement. Even at a distance I could tell it was another of them. He'd got ahead of us somehow, and was off his horse. I drew my sword as we closed on him, covering the ground in seconds. As we approached he stepped behind a tree, but he still made an easy target. I didn't manage to look back at where I hit him with the single backhand stroke of my sabre, but I'd been aiming around his head. The crack that the impact produced and the feeling of resisted penetration were quite different from what I'd have expected if my blade had simply missed and sliced into the trunk of the tree.

And yet even in that instant I had time to consider what he might have been doing; why he had scouted ahead of the others; why he had dismounted. The reason for his actions impacted my mind at the same moment it did my body: a rope stretched out between two trees, swathed in a little snow. If I'd not been distracted by the man who had constructed it, I might have seen it, but even then there would be little I could have done. The rope caught me in the dead centre of my chest. My instinct was to hang on to it, but it was impossible. Kutuzov carried on his own way, and the rope stretched and tensed and threw me back on the road behind, and all was blackness.

It was the horse who woke me. There was little enough of my face visible behind the layers of wool and linen that were wrapped around to protect it from the cold, but somehow his tongue had insinuated its way through the tiniest of gaps, and had found my nose. I sat upright. My guess was it had only been seconds since I fell, and that was confirmed when I turned and saw the Cossack who had been pursuing us approaching, now on foot. His sword was drawn. For my part, I had nothing to defend myself. My pistol wasn't loaded, and I'd dropped my sword when the rope hit me. My musket was strapped to the saddlebag, but on the far side of General Kutuzov from where I was sitting. There would be no time to get to it and then fire before the enemy reached me, but it was my only hope—and I could still make use of the bayonet, however close he was.

I waited until the man was almost upon me, and then rolled across, going beneath Kutuzov's belly and standing up on the other side of him, my hands ready to unstrap my musket. I was on the horse's right hand side now, and his mangled eye socket looked blankly at me, for a moment distracting me. The Cossack tried to come around Kutuzov's front, but I pulled at his reins, turning him so that he remained an obstacle between us. The three of us rotated through a full circle, and as we did, Kutuzov became increasingly nervous and twitchy, confused that he couldn't see me. He reared up, neighing, and kicked out with his forelegs, forcing the Cossack to take a step back.

The man changed direction and tried going around the horse's rear. Kutuzov had got into the swing of our continuous turn to the right, and I couldn't reverse it quickly enough. The Cossack passed behind Kutuzov, but must have brushed against him, however lightly. I've never seen a horse with such a kick. He threw himself onto his forelegs and both his hind legs thrust out behind him, high in the air and with huge strength.

The Cossack fell backwards onto the ground. I could hear his breath rasping. In seconds I had my musket in my hands and I approached him with the bayonet out in front of me. It looked as though one hoof had caught him in the chest, and another in the face. His nose was crushed to a pulp and he was covered with his own blood, but I could tell from the way he breathed that the injuries to his lungs were the more serious. I shoved my bayonet forwards, under his ribcage, and leaned against it. His body arched and then fell limp. I'd got him in the heart, as I'd intended. Even so, I wasn't out of trouble. His comrades were bound to be nearby and I wasn't going to wait for them to arrive.

I glanced around, but couldn't see where my sword had fallen. Instead I grabbed his. It was a strange thing, without any guard for the hand, but it would do. Kutuzov was calm again now, understanding that the immediate danger was past. I mounted him and we headed off at a trot, hoping to be away from there as quickly as possible.

We spent two more days together, not seeing a soul, until finally we hit the main road to Vilna and on it found the rearguard of the *Grande Armée*, marching dolefully towards the city. By then, General Kutuzov had eaten all the oatmeal I had to offer him. He didn't seem interested in my rice, and was happier with the potatoes, once I'd thawed them, but they wouldn't have been enough to keep me going for more than a day, let alone a huge beast like him.

Once we were on the road and amongst the infantry, there was little speed to be gained by travelling on horseback. The road was crowded, and the men were reluctant to step aside to let us pass, especially once they'd glanced up and recognized that it was a mere sergeant that towered over them. Even so, it was better to ride than to walk; I had little food left, and needed to preserve my energy.

That night we camped in the open. There was plenty of wood around, and so the whole area was lit by fires, each with groups of up to a dozen men around them. I wandered amongst the little pockets of warmth, leading Kutuzov now, until I saw a face I knew.

'Dumont?' I said.

He turned to look at me, and then frowned.

'It's me,' I continued. 'Sergeant Mellé. We were billeted together in Moscow.'

He let out a brief laugh. 'Mellé? I wouldn't have known you. You need a shave.' So did Dumont himself, but even in Moscow, he had worn a beard, so he was easier than me to recognize now. 'Join us,' he added.

I tied Kutuzov to a tree a little way away and then sat by the fire.

'That must be Harpagon,' said Dumont. I had spoken to him of my old horse many times.

'No, Harpagon died,' I replied. 'This one's called General Kutuzov.'

There was laughter all round at the name.

'It's a lucky man who has two horses during this campaign,' said one of Dumont's comrades.

'It's a lucky man whose best use for a horse is to ride it,' said another.

'What do you mean?' I asked.

'You obviously haven't been hungry,' he explained.

He was right. I'd felt hunger, but not like these men. Now I was here amongst the rearguard, I could see how badly they'd suffered. 'I have some rice,' I offered, guiltily. 'And some flour. You're welcome to share.'

'Will you share General Kutuzov?'

I looked at him. He wasn't asking for a ride. 'Never,' I said quietly.

'You're hardly in a position to keep him to yourself.'

I glanced at the figures huddled around the fire. All eyes were on me. Almost of its own volition, I felt my hand grasp the unfamiliar handle of the Cossack's sword.

'I don't think we need to be silly.' It was Dumont who spoke. 'You weren't that lucky in the Moscow Fair, were you, Mellé?' he asked. I didn't reply. I knew well enough what he meant; I'd often complained to him that it never seemed to be me who managed to unearth some treasure trove as we scrabbled through the burned down houses. But as I looked at these starving faces, knowing that I still had provisions—however meagre—in my bags, I wondered who had truly been fortunate.

Dumont began to open his knapsack. One of his comrades put out a hand to stop him, but Dumont looked at him and shrugged, and the man withdrew whatever objection he had. Dumont opened the bag. Even in the firelight, its contents glistered.

'This is our compensation for risking our lives for the Little Corporal—all of ours. We're sharing it. You could too.'

I took off my glove and reached inside, pulling out whatever caught on my fingers. The gold was icy cold, making the gems feel almost warm in contrast. I'd got hold of a couple of bracelets; one was adorned with emeralds, the other rubies. Each was probably worth enough to buy my father's whole farm. And yet it was only a fraction of what the knapsack contained.

'Take it,' hissed Dumont.

'No!' I threw the two bracelets back into the bag.

'Not enough? Name your price?' He reached in and gave me back the bracelets, then a handful of brooches and rings. Still I remained unmoved. Then he opened a side pocket and brought out the most wonderful necklace I've ever seen. 'This is our pride and joy,' he said.

'Not that!' objected the man to his right.

'What's it worth to you dead?' snapped Dumont.

The man relented, and so did I. Each of the big diamonds alone was worth enough for me to live in luxury for a decade—and there were seven of them, plus countless smaller ones. I glanced over at Kutuzov. He stood there impassively, patiently. I could tell from his stance he wasn't sleeping. I began to shovel the jewels into my own knapsack, but Dumont grabbed my wrist.

'Well?' he asked.

'You can have him,' I said.

Four of them were on their feet in an instant, heading towards the General, and he immediately sensed danger. He whinnied and reared up, pulling against his reins. If he'd wanted to he could have torn the branch from the tree and escaped.

'You're going to have to help,' said Dumont.

I stood, hoisting my knapsack onto my shoulder—I wasn't going to let go of that now—and went over. I unhooked the reins from the branch where I'd tied them and went round to the General's blind side. I knew that not being able to see me would make him more nervous. Two of the men were coming straight toward me, but I shook my head.

'Go round the back and then come at him from this side,' I said. 'It's safer.'

The two turned, and all four processed around Kutuzov's rump, making him more nervous than ever. His rear hooves were stamping into the snow, and he was making little movements from side to side. A swipe from his haunch could have knocked any one of them out. 'Calm him!' shouted one of them. I did nothing.

Then he kicked. It was Dumont that he got—right on the collar bone. I heard it crack, and he fell back onto the frozen ground. He was lucky it wasn't fatal, but with a march of five hundred leagues ahead of us, it might still have proven to be. I thrust my hand into my knapsack and grabbed the jewellery, aiming at his broken shoulder as I threw it hard back at him.

'Screw you!' I shouted. 'Kutuzov's got me this far, and I'll get him home.'

Then I took the horse's reins and led him away to some safer part of the camp, feeling a sense of pride that I hadn't known on the entire campaign.

At least…that's what I wish I could say happened. That's what I pretend when I'm lying awake at night. The truth is only a little different; just at the end.

'You're going to have to help,' said Dumont.

I stood, hoisting my knapsack onto my shoulder—I wasn't going to let go of that now—and went over. I unhooked the reins from the branch where I'd tied them and stood on the General's left, where his one eye gazed into mine. I patted his neck and he remained quite calm. Over the days we'd been together, he'd come to trust me.

'Get round the other side of him,' I said. 'He's blind in that eye.'

The four of them split into two groups, going round to the front and the back. Now he began to feel nervous. He had a better sight of the men at the front of him, so he reared up and tried to kick at them, but they kept at a safe distance. I patted him on the neck and spoke to him.

'*Ya tebya loobloo.*'

It calmed him, and at that moment, Dumont struck. He threw back his sabre and swung it hard against the creature's rear leg. It dug deep into the muscle, just above the hock. Kutuzov neighed and tried to raise the leg, but with the muscle cut, he could not. Still he managed to remain standing. Then Dumont performed the same action on the other leg, and the horse fell. His eye was wide, staring at me. His front legs scraped against the ground, desperately trying to pull his body forward. Even though he could feel the pain, he had no idea why his strong hind legs, which had served him—and me—so well in the past could not now come to his rescue.

He whinnied again and as his front hooves slipped against the hardened snow, he sank lower. I kept my head level with his, returning the look from his wide frightened eye. It was too late for there to be any need to calm him, but there was one more service I could perform to assist in his butchery. One of the men, a private, on his blind side now, approached us, bayonet in hand. With the reins in one hand and with the other under his jaw I tried to lift Kutuzov's head. But he still had enormous strength, and it was a hopeless task if he was unwilling. I patted his cheek and pleaded with him in his own language

'*Pojalsta.*'

His resistance vanished and he raised his head in the direction I was guiding it, exposing his neck. The bayonet erupted through his skin just at the level of my shoulder, forcing me to lean back rather than be injured myself. On the other side of Kutuzov I could see the excitement in the private's eyes as he put his weight against the blade. Then he began to pull forward, trying to cut Kutuzov's throat from the inside, but it was too much of a task. The horse swung his head from side to side, knocking me away, and the blade slipped out a little, only for the private to shove it back in.

'Help me, damn it!' he shouted.

With my gloved hands, it was easy enough for me to clasp the protruding end of the blade and push it forwards as the private did the same from his end. With a jerk the bayonet came out, followed by a rush of blood that spattered my arms and soaked the snow beneath.

'Don't waste that!' shouted someone, and within moments a bowl had been thrust in the way to catch the spewing blood. The private now held Kutuzov's head, but there was no more resistance from him. He was dead, or very close to it—certainly dead to the world now that no blood could reach his brain. The private's only purpose in holding him was to direct that flow of blood and make sure none was wasted. My work was done.

I went and sat back down beside the fire. Soon the others returned too. The blood from the bowl was poured into a number of small pans and cooked to make a primitive sort of *boudin noir*. The men spiked small chunks of flesh on the tips of their swords and held them in the flames to roast, but most were too hungry to wait for them to cook properly. The meat was still red and tough when they bit into it. They offered me some, but that would have been too much. Anyway, it wasn't me that was hungry. I'd never truly been hungry on the whole march.

It was only when they moved on to second helpings that they became connoisseurs.

'Anyone got any salt?' asked one.

There was a general shaking of heads.

'Try this,' said Dumont. He produced a paper cartridge and ripped the top off, throwing the ball onto the fire. Then he poured some of the black gunpowder into his hand and sprinkled it onto the man's meat. The man took a bite and nodded approvingly. Dumont seasoned his own meal in the same way, and then passed the cartridge on.

I began to inspect my rewards, hoping they would cheer me, and persuade me that what I had done was worthwhile, but there was no solace to be found there. Perhaps one day, but not now. I sifted through the smaller trinkets and found amongst them a silver brooch in the shape of a horse. From the look of it, there had once been a little gemstone mounted to represent the eye, but that was long gone. All that remained was an empty socket staring out at me.

I walked over and looked over at the remains of General Kutuzov. He was unrecognizable—bits of flesh hacked away from every part of his body; they'd taken his liver, and his kidneys, and his heart. His empty eye socket stared up at me. And then I realized—he was lying on his right hand side, and so it was his healthy left eye that I should have seen. They had taken even that.

Four days later, we arrived at Vilna and in less than two years, I was in Paris, free to spend the spoils of my campaign.

Rat-Catcher

SEANAN McGUIRE

Tybalt, you rat-catcher, will you walk?
—William Shakespeare, *Romeo and Juliet*

London, England, 1666
September

London is burning.

London is burning, and she is dead, and yet I must consider myself victorious, for others yet live. It is a cold comfort. It will have to do. How small a stretch of time stands between here, where all is ashes, and the days when I was innocent and thought myself yet young, and all the world was meant to be my stage...

July, 1666

I knew she was there.

Jill believed herself stealthy. Perhaps she would have been correct, had I not been the cat of the Duke's Theatre for four long years. I knew all the sounds that grand old building was capable of making, including the sound of a barefoot Cait Sidhe girl stalking the rafters.

"Rand!" Jill's voice came from above my head, pitched low to keep it from carrying to the audience below. She scarcely needed to bother. The evening's performance of *Romeo and Juliet* was in full swing, and no one in the theatre was looking at anything but the stage.

"*Rand!*" She sounded more insistent now, and decidedly more annoyed. I considered my responses, and decided that ignoring her would have the most amusing result. Besides, I have always loved the fight scenes.

My youngest sister dropped from the rafters to the catwalk. It was easily a nine foot drop, but she did it seemingly without effort—something she couldn't have managed even two years prior. My little Jill was growing up.

That was a sobering thought, and made it all the easier to ignore her as she stalked the length of the catwalk to the place where I sat, legs dangling. She was hissing under her breath, a habit she'd been trying, and failing, to break since kittenhood. Even so, I had little warning before she raised her hand and slapped me across the cheek. Hard. The sound had barely had time to fade before she pulled her hand back for another blow.

I raised a finger. She stopped. "You *could* do that, beloved sister of mine, and as you're faster than I am, you would likely strike me at least twice more before I dropped you on the nice mortals gathered below us. Do you think you could abandon your current shape before you hit the stage, or would your appearance be the news of all the finest taverns for the next month or so?" I turned to face her, smiling. "Either way, you'd likely be in more trouble than I would."

She hissed again, openly this time, before snapping, "You'd be the one who pushed me."

"Yes, but you would be the one who fell."

Eyes narrowed, she scowled at me. The light from the theatre below us made her look truly lovely, with her milk-pale skin and her fog-colored hair, banded down its length with darker stripes of gray. I have always thought tabby girls were the prettiest kind.

"I hate you."

"I know."

She sat with a huff, not bothering to look down; she simply trusted that the catwalk would be where she wanted it to be. "I truly, truly *hate* you," she said, adopting a cross-legged pose that hiked her layered skirts up past her knees in a way the mortals would call indecent.

"So you do, my darling Jill, so you do, but you love me none the less for it." I leaned forward to get a better view of the action below, keeping my hands braced on the catwalk for balance. "I do love the way they stage the duels here."

"You've seen this show a dozen times!"

"Closer to a dozen dozens, more likely, and yet I never tire of it." I glanced away from the actors long enough to grin at her. "Can't you relax for one evening, and enjoy a little entertainment?"

"No, I can't, and neither should you." Jill folded her arms. Her pupils were open to their fullest, reducing her brilliant orange irises to rings. She looked utterly, unrepentantly fae. This high above the mortal crowd, there was no point to masquerading as one of their number. "Father wants you."

"So he sent you to retrieve me? Did he consider, for a moment, that I might refuse to come?"

"He did, yes."

"And?"

"And if I fail to retrieve you, I'm to be put to work minding the kittens for a week's time, to teach me obedience." Her scowl could have frightened Oberon himself. "I won't mind kittens for *you*, Rand. You're coming with me, whether you like it or not."

"Am I, then?" I raised an eyebrow, looking at her. "Will you fight me in order to bring me home? Much as I love you, darling Jill, I doubt you'd come out the winner in that particular contest."

"I won't fight you."

"Then what?"

"I'll sit here and cry through your precious performance if you refuse to come. And tomorrow night, when my time in the nursery ends, I'll do the same. And the night after that, and the night after that, until such time as you apologize to me." Jill smiled sweetly. "You can save us both a great deal of time and suffering if you simply come with me now."

I cast a longing look toward the actors. Mercutio was preparing to die, and in the process was layering curses down on both the warring houses. "Are you quite sure Father can't wait?"

"Come *on*." Jill flowed to her feet with the sort of boneless grace that only Cait Sidhe girls possess, grabbing my arm and tugging as she tried to make me follow. "You know how it ends, Rand. The girl dies. The boy dies. Everyone dies. They're mortals, that's what they *do*."

"I suppose that's true enough." I climbed to my feet, more slowly than she had, and followed her along the catwalk toward the wall. I only glanced back twice; a personal best for leaving while the stage was in use. "Everyone dies."

If anyone in the audience looked up, they would have seen only two tabby cats, one black and brown, one white and gray, climbing up the curtains that hung around the highest of the theatre windows and vanishing out into the night. So far as I know, no one looked.

⁂

Jill remained in her four-legged form until we were three full rooftops away from the Duke's Theatre. Then, with a graceful twist and the smell of silver birch and crushed chalk, she was two-legged again. "You *must* stop running off like this, Rand!" she scolded, planting her hands on her hips for emphasis. It was intended to make her look stern. In actuality, it made me want to ruffle her ears and tell her she was endearing when angry. "Father is furious, and when he's furious, it's us that suffer, not you. It's unfair, is what it is."

My own magic rose around me, scenting the air with penny-royal and musk. I stood and looked at her mildly, stretching as I rolled my shoulders into place. She scowled. With Jill, it was best to be mild as milk and sweet as honey—she couldn't stand it, and anything which drove her to distraction couldn't help delighting me.

"I don't see why you should suffer for my misbehaviors, sweet Jill," I said, widening my eyes in a parody of sincerity. I saw enough of it in my actors; why shouldn't I take a lesson or two from them? "I shall tell Father straightaway."

"And he will put you through a wall just as quickly, leaving us to tend your wounds." Jill glared before turning to stalk away across the roof, her skirts swishing around her ankles.

I followed at an easy pace. There were two chimneys, one hot from the fire it hosted, and one long cooled. Jill stopped at the second chimney, shooting a final glare in my direction before grabbing the edge and hoisting herself up.

"You're coming this time?" she asked.

"I am right behind you; you have my word."

"Worth the paper it's not printed on," she grumbled, shifting to her feline form before leaping into the flue and disappearing.

Laughing, I took two steps back, and then ran at the chimney, shifting forms at the last possible moment. As a cat, I fell through the darkness and out of the realm of mortal London, descending into the Court of Cats.

※

The Court of Cats exists in the tenuous membrane between the Summerlands and every other realm of mortal or Faerie. As such, it belongs to none of them and all of them, all at the same time. Passage is through the shadows which are the burden and birthright of the Cait Sidhe. In London, those shadows were kept open by the will of the King, Ainmire, who had held dominion over our Court for nigh two centuries.

The shadows were cold. I breathed shallowly as I fell, trying to feel the edges of our route. My efforts were to no avail; the shadows remained as thick and secretive as they always did. I still had much to learn about the Shadow Roads. Jill was more adept at their manipulation, despite having only sixteen years to my twenty. By the time I fell back into the light and shifted to a more human form, she was nowhere to be seen.

The hall which connected to the chimney we had used for passage was broad, apparently hewn from solid oak. I sniffed one of the walls, curiously. It smelled of wood smoke and pitch. "Viking construction," I said. "Really, Jill. Too simple."

"You still had to check," she said, stepping out of a shadow to my left. I turned toward the sound of her voice, and thus my back was entirely unprotected when Colleen slammed into me, her hands going straight for my throat. Jill yawned. "Too simple."

I would have answered her, but was preoccupied with the effort of keeping my older sister from throttling the life out of my body. I managed to twist around and catch her by the back of the neck, grabbing tightly. She struggled to be free, and I obliged her, releasing her neck and giving her a shove for good measure. She snarled as she stumbled backward, recovering her balance before shifting her weight onto her toes and leaping once more. I was more prepared this time, and stepped to the side, allowing her to slam into the wall. The impact mashed her lips back against her teeth, bloodying them.

Colleen raised a hand to her mouth, pulling it away and looking narrow-eyed at the blood on her fingers. Then she turned to smile at me, revealing bloody teeth and oversized incisors. "Very *good*, little brother," she said. "Maybe we won't be spending another week by your bedside after all."

I sighed. "Hello, Colleen, you look lovely this evening, it's always such a pleasure to share the loving bosom of my family with such a glorious sister. To what do I owe the honor of your attack?"

"Father is angry," she replied, lowering her hand. "I grow tired of covering for you."

"Yet you do it all the same." I smiled at her. Colleen scowled in response. I had long suspected that she and I came from the same mother, although Father would, of course, never confirm something so common as lineage. She was calico-patterned, with blocks of black and orange skin carrying over even into her human form, and her eyes were a sweet, clear shade of green. There was a certain similarity to our features, once the differences of gender and coloration were accounted for.

"You'll be the death of us," she snapped. Stepping forward, she looped her arm through mine. Jill did the same on my opposite side. "No more running."

"Not tonight," I agreed, affably enough.

Still scowling, my sisters pulled me down the hall, and toward the inevitable.

In my twenty years, I had never seen a Court of Cats outside of mortal London, or the fae Kingdom of Londinium. As such, I did not know whether they were all controlled by fear and rage. What little I'd heard from the cats who passed through with traveling humans caused me to believe that some Courts might, in fact, be kinder places for a kit who dreamt of things more fanciful than simple power. Not that it would have mattered if every other Court of Cats was a paradise second only to Tirn Ailil itself. The Court of Fogbound Cats was my home, and it was that Court's King who I and my sisters called Father.

Jill and Colleen released my arms as the three of us shifted to our four-legged forms, the better to navigate the narrow rigging connecting the throne room to the rest of the Court. Father's assemblies were conducted in what was once the hold of a Spanish sailing galleon, before it was sunk in the mortal world and drifted into the Court of Cats, where all lost things go. How it came into Father's possession was a mystery to me, and likely to remain so. There was much he did not choose to tell me, nor ever would.

Jars filled with captive witch-light were studded around the room seemingly at random, providing illumination for our changeling cousins while also leaving shadows for the rest of us to come and go as we pleased. Father was seated in his throne at the head of the room, as he so often was, with two of his current doxies competing for possession of his lap. One was a pretty calico who looked too much like Colleen for comfort; the other had the dark hands and pale complexion of the Siamese, with the bright blue eyes to match.

Those blue eyes cast a measuring glance in our direction as my sisters and I stood, stretching feline limbs into human lankiness. Her nose wrinkled, and she turned her head to murmur in my father's ear, the cant of her chin telegraphing her displeasure as plainly as a twitching tail.

Whatever result she'd been hoping for, I doubt it was the one she got. Father raised his head, eyes narrowing to baleful slits. Then he stood, sending the women sprawling as he stalked toward us. I smiled, stepping forward to meet him.

"Hello, Father. My dear sister was kind enough to inform me that you—"

His hand closed around my throat, cutting off most of my air supply. I forced myself to keep smiling as he jerked me toward him, snarling into my face, "You were bid to be present when the sun went down. The sun has been down for some time. How do you answer this?"

I coughed, endeavoring to look piteous. It wasn't as difficult as it might have been; the lack of oxygen was beginning to make my lungs ache. He dropped me, hissing in disgust.

"I was otherwise engaged," I said, rubbing my throat and making no effort to rise. To do so too quickly would just result in his slapping me down again. "I apologize for my delinquency. To what do I owe the honor of this summons?"

Father glared. I looked innocently back, the very picture of the faithful Prince awaiting the word of his King. It's a look I have had great occasion to cultivate, since I desired neither challenge nor exile.

I had two brothers, once. They were not so good as I at playing the foolish son—and until such time as Father found a younger brother to bear home to my sisters and I, he would no more press me to challenge him than I would rush the moment.

"You are to go to the Divided Courts," spat Father, finally. "An envoy has been requested for the latest of their assemblies. To show respect, I must send a member of the family. To show scorn, I am sending them *you*."

"Your faith in me will not go unrewarded, Father!" I caroled, bounding to my feet with as much vigor as I could muster. My throat ached, but I would not show weakness; not here, not with him watching my every move. "When shall I depart?"

His smile was terrible to behold. "That is why I summoned you at sunset, my dear boy. They expect you at any moment. You will have to travel the shadows—and you will have to do so on your own."

He turned away, walking back to his throne and the waiting arms of his doxies. When I turned, my sisters would not meet my eyes. All too aware of what awaited me, I raised my chin and walked out of the throne room.

❧❦

My first passage through the shadows occurred when I was eight years of age, still a kitten finding my feet. My father, in his infinite wisdom, opened the door to the Shadow Roads, threw me through the opening, and closed the door again. It was the last of the trials intended to prove that I was, indeed, a Prince of Cats, and not merely another mouth for him to trouble himself feeding.

Colleen found me in a London alleyway three hours later, unconscious, half-frozen, and naked. It was a blessing that I'd not been found by the city's mortal populace as I lay there, clearly inhuman, and just as clearly defenseless. But I had survived; that was what mattered. I was named a potential heir to Father's Court the very next day, and the torment commenced in earnest. Ah, well; it was better than the alternatives.

The shadows in the hall slid open under my hand, and I stepped into the biting cold, trying desperately to command the path to open ahead of me. This was nothing so simple as navigating the comparatively comfortable and well-traveled path between the rooftops of London and the Court of Cats; this was a branch of the Shadow Roads that was little enough walked to be balky, and to make me yearn for Jill's advanced skill as I held my breath and plunged through the dark.

After what seemed an interminable amount of time, the shadows parted in front of me, and I stepped out, shivering, onto the polished marble floor of the royal knowe. The air smelled of sweet posies, and windows on every wall afforded a clear view of the starlit Summerlands sky. I walked with as much grace as I could muster to the nearest of those windows, sitting down upon the sill while I waited for the ache in my lungs to abate.

"I am here, and not eternally lost in frozen darkness," I said, philosophically. "Things can always be worse."

"True, but can they be more amusing?"

The voice was female and familiar. I smiled despite the ache in my chest as I turned. "My lady. I would bow, but at the moment, I fear it would land me on either my head or my tail, with no way to predict which would suffer greater damage."

"As your lack of brain will necessitate your trading upon your looks for most of your life, I suggest your tail." The owner of the voice was a tall, slender Daoine Sidhe with shockingly red hair and eyes yellow enough to have caused me to tease her, on several occasions, about her clear Cait Sidhe ancestry. She had none, more's the pity; she would have made a fabulous cat.

We met when circumstance caused me to pursue a mouse into her bedchambers. It's rare that a woman makes her first impression upon me with a broom handle to my skull, but that was September. Rare, indeed, especially for a lady of the Daoine Sidhe. She was the best of them.

"My lady's will be done." I stood, offering her my hands. "My sweet September. I have counted the seconds we were apart."

"Please don't let my husband hear you say that," she said, taking my hands in hers and squeezing them lightly. "Come along, Rand. The court has already been called to order, and your tardiness reflects poorly on your father."

"What a shame," I said blandly, and allowed her to lead me down the hall to the royal receiving room.

The Court of Cats is made up of the world's lost things, rooms and halls and narrow spaces stitched together with enchantments too ancient to see. The knowe of the King and Queen of Londinium was something altogether different, a vast palace beyond the wildest dreams of any mortal regent. It was one of the oldest knowes in all of Britain, and it carried a weight of history that was impressive even by the standards of the fae. Being a cat, I strolled along as if I was not impressed in the least.

"What is this about, this summons?" I asked. "Have your brothers been naughty again? I would be pleased to stand witness to their banishment."

"Nothing so pleasant for you, I'm afraid." September looked at me, the levity gone from her eyes. "The Undersea has sent an ambassador, but he has refused to present his message to the court until a representative of every fief and household in the city proper was present—including the Court of Cats."

I frowned. "That's troublesome, and quite strange, but I do not see the gravity."

"The ambassador is Merrow. The message is Roane."

"Ah." I swallowed, wishing my human form had a tail that I could lash in my dismay. "I suppose we had best hurry, then."

"Yes," September agreed. "We had best."

෨෩෪

Of the Roane, only three things need be known: that they see the future, but never clearly; that few of them remain among the living; and that the one disaster they did not foretell was the one which killed the greater part of their number. Some believe they saw even that coming, and decided to allow it, believing that the loss of their lives would balance out some greater tragedy ahead. Perhaps I am a selfish man, but I cannot believe they knew what was coming and chose to simply let it happen.

What few Roane remained after the slaughter were taken in by the courts of the Undersea, where they have been cosseted and protected as prophets ever since. For a Roane to be sent to the land was near unprecedented…and while I may be young,

I have yet to encounter anything that was both unprecedented and pleasant.

September raised a finger to her lips, signaling for quiet as we reached the throne room doors. Two pages in royal livery waited there, both Tylwyth Teg. They bowed and opened the doors, allowing us to slip inside and join the crowd already assembled. September had spoken the truth. There were over twenty independent fiefdoms within the city of London alone, and at least twice that many people occupied the room, looking as anxious and unsettled as actors gathered for a first rehearsal. The King and Queen would be the theatre's patrons, then, sitting on their thrones with the bulk of the assembly before them. That left the director's role for the shark-eyed Merrow standing in front of the thrones. A slip of a girl with hair the color of a seal's pelt hung from his hand like a rag, barely supporting her own weight.

The King raised his head when the door swung closed. His lips pressed together in a hard line as he saw me. "The Court of Cats has finally seen fit to grace us with a guest," he said, and looked to the Merrow. "Might you tell us now why you have come? We are consumed with curiosity."

From the murmuring of the assembled, it was plain the King did not employ the royal "we" in this instance. Everyone here wanted to know, myself included. I slipped away from September, working my way through the crowd with a cat's skill. In only a few moments, I was near the front, where I could better see the Merrow and his silver-haired companion.

"We have come at the bidding of King Murtagh, who has long appreciated the relationship between Londinium and his own lands, and who wished to send a warning to you while warnings might still do some good." The Merrow addressed his words, not to the King and Queen, but to the crowd. Interesting, that.

"And what is this 'warning'?" asked the King, barely keeping the annoyance from his tone.

"A moment, sire." The Merrow turned to the waif who dangled from his hand, crouching to look through the curtain of her hair. "Naia? It's time to speak now, dear heart, and then we can go home. You'd like that, wouldn't you? To go home?"

The Roane girl nodded, so slightly that it might have been only a tremble. Then she raised her head, turning startlingly green eyes on the room. She looked as if she only half-saw us. The rest of her gaze was far away, looking at something I was grateful not to see.

"The waves will keep us safe," she said, in a faltering voice. "The land has no such merciful protection."

"That's true, my dear," he said. "Can you tell the land what they need protection from?"

"Ah." She stood up a little straighter, brushing the hair from her face with her free hand. Gaze suddenly focusing on the present, she said, "The fires will come, and though many will run, few will survive the burning. In their wake will come sickness such as has never been seen before nor will be seen again, and it will be a second burning, one that kills without concern for fae or mortal bloodlines. Few who call Londinium home will survive those fires, and royal lines will be henceforth shattered into history and dust."

The room went completely silent as she spoke, all but holding its collective breath. Naia looked from face to face, expression thoughtful.

"I have seen many of you before, in the motion of the water," she said finally. "Too many have I seen on night-haunt wings. Flee this land while the future can yet be changed. Stay, and may the mercy of the waters be upon you." The clarity fled her eyes, and she turned back to her companion, whimpering, "Can we go home now? Please? This place is too dry, and too vast, and set too soon by far to burn."

"Yes, dear one, we can go. You have done well." The Merrow twisted to look at the King and Queen. "Three seers have brought the same vision to our King. Fires, and sickness, such as will kill whomever remains here. If you would save your people, evacuate and leave your lands. If you will not do so…then may Oberon have mercy, for the flames, I fear, will not."

The crowd parted to let the Merrow and his companion walk from the room, Naia leaning on him like he was the only thing keeping her upright. The silence lasted only until the pair had left the room. Then the gathering erupted, everyone demanding answers, information, reassurance—all things the King and Queen, being as stunned as the rest of us, were hard-pressed to give.

I made my way through the crowd back to September, who was standing frozen beside the doors. "I should carry this news home, and quickly," I said. "Will you be well?"

September laughed uncomfortably. "I will tell Malcolm it's time to visit his family in Wales. He'll be delighted, I'm sure. Don't worry for me, Sir Cat." She reached out, grabbing one of my hands in both of hers, and smiled. "I'm a Torquill. No matter what, we survive. We're frankly annoying in that regard."

"See to it that you do," I commanded, and pulled my hand from hers. The room behind me still alive with outraged voices, I slipped out into the hall and began to make my way toward home.

Fear is a great motivator, and urgency a great enhancer of skill. My journey back to the Court of Cats was only half so difficult as the journey outward had been, and I felt barely chilled when I stepped out of the shadows. I was in another of our endlessly interchangeable halls, this one stone-walled, with tattered tapestries adding little warmth. I stopped before I'd taken three full steps, raising my head and sniffing the air. Then I sighed.

"Please come out," I said. "This is not the time, and my nerves are too frayed by far to be a pleasant opponent in a game of catch-the-mouse."

"You're no fun when you're serious," declared Colleen, stepping from behind one of the tapestries. Then she frowned, pupils narrowing. "You're pale. Rand, are you well? What ails you?"

"Is Jill here?" I looked around the hall again, consumed with the sudden need to see the both of my sisters alive and well. "Jill, come out. I have no patience for games."

A tabby cat slunk out of the shadows at the base of one wall, and stood, resolving itself into my sister. Her frown melted into a look of concern that mirrored Colleen's. "Brother?"

I stepped forward, grabbing each of them with one arm and sweeping them into a crushing three-part embrace. Jill squeaked, sounding almost like a kitten herself. Then they both embraced me back, purring soothingly. I buried my face in their shoulders, breathing in the reassuring scent of them, Jill's crushed chalk and silver birch, Colleen's thistles and juniper. Dimly, I realized that my shoulders were slumped, the sheer terror of the Roane's prediction pressing down on them like leaden weights.

London, and Londinium, were to burn. Whatever disaster was ahead of the city, the normal delineation between worlds would not protect those of us who lived there.

"Rand, what's *wrong*?" asked Colleen.

I pulled away from their embrace, keeping hold of their arms as I studied their faces. They looked back at me, wide-eyed and bewildered.

"If I told you that we had to run, leave this Court and flee as far as legs would carry us, would you go?" I asked, urgently. "Would you trust me, and follow me, and not ask why?"

Colleen raised her hand, rubbing its edge along my cheek. "You know we couldn't. Father would find us, and the punishment would be worse than whatever fate you had us flee."

I sighed. "Would that I were half so sure as you." I stepped back, letting the pair of them go. "I must go meet with Father. Will you attend?"

"Gladly," said Jill, offering her hand. Colleen did the same, and hand in hand, the three of us walked down the hall, toward the room where the King our father was waiting.

⚘

Luck, of a kind, was with us; after all the importance Father had placed on my going to the Court of Londinium without delay, he had chosen to show his own disdain for their message by disappearing on some errand of his own. The throne room was deserted. I walked to his throne, placing a hand upon the cushion softening it. The fabric was cool. He had been gone for some time; possibly even as long as I had. I bit back a curse, stepping back and turning to face Jill and Colleen. They hung back some feet away, watching me with wary eyes.

"Where is he?"

"Father no more reports his movements to us than you to him," said Jill. "What is this? Why do you fret and not speak of the reasons?"

"Be kind, Jill. His message may be for his King's ears only."

Jill hissed, cuffing Colleen hard across the face. Colleen hissed back, but didn't hit her. Jill raised her hand again, bobbing it in the air like she might strike.

I sighed. "Amusing as this is, this is not the time."

Now the looks they turned toward me were baffled, like I had suddenly declared my intent to sever all ties with the Court of Cats and join the Cu Sidhe in their baying at the moon. "Brother, are you well?" asked Colleen.

"No." I shook my head. "I am not well at all. Father bound you to fetch me to him once before; I beg you, do the same again. When he returns, come for me. I must speak to him, and I must do my speaking soon."

"Where will you be?" asked Colleen.

"Where I always am, when there are things I should rather avoid." A faint smile tugged at my lips. "I'm going to the theatre."

The night's performance was long over, the crowd dispersed back into the London streets. The sound of voices drifted from the rear of the stage, where some of the cast and crew had doubtless gathered for a laugh before returning to the hovels they called home. Ah, the glamorous life of the theatre. I walked in that direction with my tail held high and my ears pricked forward, confident that my compatriots would sense nothing of my distress in my demeanor. They were only human, after all.

The Cait Sidhe, more than almost any other breed of fae, have always co-existed with humanity. There's some question as to whether man domesticated the cat, or whether the Cait Sidhe domesticated man and decided to share the spoils with our little mortal cousins. Whatever the reality, the truth of the matter is that where there are men, there have always been cats, and cream, and Cait Sidhe hiding their true nature behind a purr.

The first to spot me was Dick Allington, the company's erstwhile director. "Look! Tom's come to cast approval on our performance!" he roared, saluting my entrance with his flask. "Were we successful, old boy? Did we pack the stalls with feet enough to kick loose some tasty rats for your supper?"

I walked over to him, stopping some three feet distant. There I sat, wrapping my tail about my legs, and miaowed as piteously as I could. The men laughed.

"No rats for Old Tom tonight, Dicky! I told you the second act needed work!" Peter Skelling was a man of all roles and a master of none. He'd played near every part the theatre held title to, and done them all diffidently well, with nothing to either shame or recommend him. There was something to be said for a man who devoted so much time and energy to being unrelentingly average.

"Then it will have to be cream and cold chicken again, eh, Tom?" Dick leaned forward to scratch beneath my chin. I closed my eyes, submitting to the familiarity. After so many years in this theatre, these men were owed at least that much from me.

The thought was almost laughable in its absurdity. A Cait Sidhe, owing anything to a human? It was unthinkable. And yet it was so, and I would have done anything to spare them from what was yet to come.

Anything but break the veil of silence that stood between Faerie and the mortal world. There are things too precious to be broken for the sake of a room full of mortal men.

"Here, sir," said a voice—young, barely broken, the human equivalent of a half-grown kitten. I turned, opening my eyes. Young Tom, the boy who played the company's female roles and children, knelt beside me, setting two dishes on the floor. One held the promised chicken; the other, milk, instead of cream. Close enough, considering I had come to say farewell. I moved toward the dishes, bending my head toward the chicken.

Tom dared a scratch behind my ears as I ate. I did not protest, but hunkered down to eat, tail-tip twitching. The men roared laughter once again.

"He's finally learning to love you as we do, Tommy," said Peter. "Why, that's the first time I've seen you touch Old Tom without paying blood for the privilege."

I flattened one ear, making it plain that I was listening. The men continued talking, blissfully unaware that I could understand them.

The chicken was plain but pleasant; the milk, slightly sour, but drinkable all the same. I ate perhaps half of each before rising, stretching my back into an eloquent crescent, and beginning to make my rounds of the room. Half the company was here, at best, but it would have to do, for I could not risk this again.

At each man, I stopped, butted my head against knees or shins, and then miaowed loudly. They laughed and commented on how affectionate I was, none of them knowing that what I said, over and over, was "You must leave London at once. Please, friends, while there is still time."

When my circuit brought me back to Dick, I leapt lightly into his lap and stood, my rear paws on his knee and my forepaws on his chest. He laughed. I patted his cheek with one paw, claws carefully velveted, and miaowed again.

"Oh, you're a good lad, Tom. A theatre is only as good as its cat, I say." Dick's hand caressed my ears with the ease of long practice. I set up a rumbling purr, dropping back to his lap and folding myself into a loaf. These men, who had never exchanged a word with me and knew nothing of my place or station…these men were some of the truest friends I had ever known.

I remained where I was until a burst of laughter from Peter caused me to open my eyes and turn to look at him. "Tom, you old rascal, you didn't tell us you had such pretty girlfriends waiting for you!" He was pointing to the door, where two cats—one a delicate tabby, the other a larger, but still lovely, calico—sat, tails wrapped around their legs, looking at us.

Colleen miaowed. Only once, but that was all that I required. I stood, stretching languidly, and butted my head one last time against Dick's chest before jumping down and walking to my sisters. The men laughed, Dick calling, "Off home to the wives, eh, Tom? Hope you've been well-behaved, for I'd hate to see a cat put into the dog's house!"

The sound of their laughter followed us out of the theatre. They had been my friends; they had been the best of humanity. I had killed a hundred rats to please them; I had viewed near as many performances on that lonely stage. And I would never see any of them again.

❦

We made our way back to the rooftops before resuming our human forms, the mingled scents of our magic mixing with the sweet decay of the London summer night. Colleen turned to face me, walking backward along the edge of the roof.

"Father returned in a temper," she said. "He did not expressly send us to retrieve you and may well be angry over our absence by now. I hope you have reason for what you do tonight, Rand, and are not merely trying to be troublesome."

"I always have reasons for my actions, dear sister," I said.

"Then why to the theatre? Why back to your human pets?"

"I had to say goodbye to them."

Jill cast me a startled, wide-eyed glance. Colleen looked at me appraisingly before she turned to face our destination, walking normally once more. Neither of them said anything as we walked, and I allowed the silence to hold. There was nothing here for any of us to say.

The shadows seemed to part a trifle easier this time, perhaps because I was too tired to fight against them. We emerged just outside the throne room door, Colleen a few steps before me, Jill the same distance behind. Neither of them attacked as I straightened, caught my breath, and walked toward the door. They knew as well as I did that this was not the time, even if they were not so clear as to the reasons why.

I hesitated at the doorway, wondering if there was any other way than this. Could I take my sisters and follow September and her husband to his homeland, far from Londinium? I'd played at theatre's cat, and to play at housecat would not be so great a stretch. We would be safe. We would be in the company of friends.

We would be traitors, and while we might yet be cats, we would no longer be Cait Sidhe. I breathed slowly out, and opened the door.

Father's doxies were not in evidence; nor were the other members of his Court. The silence was almost palpable as I walked in, my sisters behind me. Our feet made no sound. My oldest brother used to stomp when he walked, more human than feline, no matter how often Father tried to beat it out of him. I had barely thought of Carr in years—not since the day he challenged for the Kingship, and lost. The room had been just this quiet on that day, when it was his turn to walk toward the throne, and five of us stood arrayed behind him.

Cailin paid the price of his transgression, pretty little Cailin, with her black and white fur and her smile like the morning. Would it be Jill or Colleen who paid the price of mine?

"Hello, Father." My words fell into the silence like stones. "I must speak with you. It is a matter of some grave importance."

He raised his head, expression calculating. "You overreach yourself, kit. I choose what holds importance in this Court."

"You sent me to hear a message."

"Is that what I sent you to do? I thought I sent you to silence the whining of the Divided Courts and buy me peace. Peace which you are now disrupting."

I took a slow breath, silently begging Oberon for strength. Then, carefully, I said, "The Undersea sent an ambassador who tended to their message—tended, not tendered, for she was a Roane girl, and not some simple proclamation." The first spark of interest came into his eyes. I continued: "She said the city was to burn, and all of Londinium with it. The division of the worlds will not protect us. We must flee, Father. That is what the Roane's vision told her, and what she carried here, to us. We must flee, or surely we will burn." And those who did not burn would face a death even less forgiving. He had to see the sense of flight. He had to understand—

There was no warning before he struck. Ainmire had been King too long for that. One moment, he was in his throne and the next, he was slamming me to the ground. I had barely seen him move. He placed a foot against my chest, pinning me down, and roared, more lion than housecat. I struggled to free myself, scrabbling uselessly at his ankle.

"*You do not dictate here!*" he snarled, and bent, taking his foot away before he grabbed me by my shoulders, claws piercing skin and flesh through the fabric of my shirt and waistcoat. "*I* am King! *I* say whether we stand or run! *I* protect us, and no fire will drive me from my Kingdom!" He shook me, claws digging deeper. "*Do you understand?*"

I looked into the yellow-ringed darkness of his eyes, and saw that there was no reasoning with him. Still, I had to try. Struggling to keep my voice level despite the pain, I said, "You are King, Father, but the fire will not care. The Roane are never wrong. If we stay, we *will* burn."

"As long as I am King, we stay." He dropped me, hard, like he would discard a piece of garbage. "What do you say to that, kitten?"

I closed my eyes.

Kings and Queens of Cats are made, yes, but Princes and Princesses are born. Only some Cait Sidhe have the power required to take the throne, and much to the annoyance of our rulers, very few of us breed true. So far as I knew, all of the kittens Ainmire had been able to sire had been Cait Sidhe, pure and simple—rare things, to be sure, but not nobility in waiting.

Without challengers to come from within, he left himself open to challenge from without. No roving King would challenge a Court with a Prince who might yet take it. So our father, in his wisdom, spent years purchasing potential heirs. Three boys to challenge for his throne, none trained to win it. Three girls, to hold those boys in check, and remind them of the consequences of their actions.

Cailin died when Carr failed his challenge for the throne. Arles chose exile over battle, leaving me with two hostages to my name: Jill, and Colleen. For their sake, I had never dared come this close to challenge.

For their sake, I had no other choice.

"I say, Father, that I am no longer a kitten." I opened my eyes, smiling as blithely as I could while my stomach shriveled to a solid knot of fear. "Nor, I am afraid, are you a King."

I launched myself at him almost before I finished speaking. He roared, swatting me aside. It was reflex as much as anything, and reflex which acted in my favor; rather than getting scratched more badly than I already was, I simply went sprawling, scrambled to my feet, and leapt again.

The rules of chivalry and gentle conduct belong to the Divided Courts, and not to the Court of Cats. We respect only blood.

This time, Father let me hit him, digging my claws deep into the muscle of his chest. His hand closed around the back of my neck, yanking me loose and shaking me hard until my teeth rattled. I kicked at his belly, rear claws extending as I sliced and tore. The smell of his blood filled the air, hot and copper-bright. He roared again, slamming me to the floor so hard that something snapped in my chest. His foot caught me in the belly, digging into the soft tissue there.

"Kitten," he spat. "Boy. *Weakling*. I let you live this long because of that, but you're no more heir than your brothers were." I hissed weakly, trying to rise. He kicked me again, knocking the last of the wind from my lungs. I sank back to the floor. "What am I to do with you? Hmm?" He knelt down so I could see his face, and smiled. "I know. Sleep well, little prince. You have failed me for the last time."

His hand caught me in the middle of my chest, and before I realized what he was doing, I was falling into the endless cold dark of the Shadow Roads. A glimmer of light above me exposed the door he had opened to push me through…and then that slammed with the finality of an executioner's axe coming down, and all was dark, and cold.

I do not know how long I fell. Only that the dark seemed endless, and that nothing stopped me falling. Finally, I forced myself to stretch a hand into the black, and grab the edge of a doorway I told myself was there. My fall continued a few seconds more before my fingers hit something solid, jerking the rest of me to a halt. I hung there, suspended and surprised.

Then I began climbing back up.

My ribs were aching, and the pain in my stomach was worse. I continued to climb, focusing on getting to someone who could help. The Cait Sidhe harm. We do not heal. Jill and Colleen needed me to get back to them—needed me to finish challenging Father, before he…before…

I pulled myself further up, reached out, and opened a door out of darkness, into light.

September looked up from the trunk she was packing, eyes going wide as I stumbled out of her wardrobe. I attempted to say something witty to put her mind at ease—anything at all—but the words refused to come. I hit the floor a moment later, and fell into a second, much warmer, darkness.

※

The pain in my ribs was gone when I woke, as were my clothes. I was tucked into a large bed, with a goose feather duvet stretched across me. I sat up, stretched, and rose, heading out in search of my hostess—or, failing that, my clothing.

I met September halfway down the hall, a bundle of clothing in her arms. She stopped when she saw me. "I see you're awake," she said, after a moment's uncomfortable silence.

I bowed. "I am, and feeling much the better. Your gracious hospitality is a true credit to your court. Now, if I might be reunited with my trousers, I truly must be going. Not that modesty moves me, but there is something of a draft within the shadows, and I prefer to be covered."

Wordlessly, she held her bundle of clothing out to me. I took it, noting without surprise that my waistcoat was gone. The tears from Father's claws were doubtless too great to be repaired. "You are too kind to a wayward fool," I said gravely, and bowed again before beginning to dress.

September found her voice as I tied the front of my trousers, saying, "What is going *on*, Rand? You fell from nowhere."

"Ah." I glanced up at her. "I fell from the shadows, where I was thrown upon failing to kill my father. I'm afraid there's no choice in the matter now. I must kill him or let all the Court of Fogbound Cats burn. I do appreciate your hospitality, my lady. You are the best of your kind."

"Rand—" She took a step forward, one hand out, as if to reach for me. Then she stopped, realizing who she was, who *I* was, and pulled her hand away. "Good luck, my friend."

I mustered a smile. "There is no luck, lady. But your wishes warm my heart. Now fly before the flames arrive." I turned, not letting myself look back—looking back has never brought anything but misfortune and pain—as I parted the shadows at the base of the nearest wall and stepped into the dark.

For the first time, the shadows did not fight me. I had faced them without fear, fought through them to a chosen destination, and now, at last, they conceded my authority. I ran through darkness, cutting through the space between the Lady Torquill's halls and the Court of my father. In what seemed like only seconds, I was bursting back out into the world.

I landed on my feet, surrounded by a stunned ring of Cait Sidhe. "Father! Face me!"

The man at the room's far end turned slowly, revealing the grave face of the man who bought me, raised me, and played the only parent I had ever known. I caught the briefest glimpse of the figure before him as he moved. She was pale and unmoving, and I did not need to see her face; her hair was like the London fog. My heart died a little in that moment.

"She did nothing wrong," I half-whispered.

"She failed to counsel you to patience," Ainmire replied. "She was never fit to be a Queen."

"She was my sister, and I loved her."

"Then you should have thought before you struck me." He began to circle, setting the edges of what would be our battleground. The Cait Sidhe fell back, opening space. None would interfere. Not here; not with this. "You knew what you did. You did it all the same."

"If we stay here, all of us will die."

"How would you know that? The mortal world has burned before, and the seal-kin are not of our kind. Their prophecies do not bind us." He raised a hand, claws extended and gleaming in the witch-light. "The world can always do with fewer human rats."

"She was my *sister*," I repeated, and leapt. Not toward him—into the darkness. The shadows opened for my passage, closing behind me.

Father's frustrated roars still echoed through the room when I slipped out of the shadows, now feline-formed and clinging to the high beams close to the ceiling. I kept low as I slunk along, waiting until I was close to the wall before miaowing, loudly, and leaping into the shadows once more.

I emerged in the room's furthest corner, and watched as Father transformed himself into a cat and scrambled up the nearest tapestry to the rafters. He stalked along, snarling. I straightened on two legs, cupped my mouth, and called, "Hadn't you best kill me quick, Father? Your subjects will begin to question your command."

He turned, hissing. I dove back into the darkness.

I expected to tire. I expected him to follow me onto the Shadow Roads, catch me by the throat, and break my body against the dark. Neither happened. My fear and anxiety were gone, replaced by a cold core of anger. He would endanger his subjects for nothing but his pride, and his unwillingness to risk losing his Court. A fair concern, but not worth a single life. He backed me into the need to challenge him, and Jill—ah, Jill, my darling girl—paid the cost of his machinations. Nothing I could do this day would bring her back to me.

Navigating him into the desired position took what felt like hours, but was doubtless only minutes. I was a theatre cat. I knew the importance of blocking. When he stepped into the center of the room, below the point where once the sailors hung their nets to dry, I saw my cue, and I took it.

My drop from the rafters onto his back caught him off-guard. He snarled and grabbed for me, but my arm was already locked around his neck, and my knees against the sides of his ribcage. He struggled, magic gathering as he prepared to shift forms. I tightened my grip, hissing in his ear, "I will snap your neck if you become smaller than I am. Concede, Father. Do not make me kill you."

His roar was muffled by the lack of air. Choking, he stumbled forward, one hand outstretched, while the other clawed at my arm, seeking purchase. I squeezed tighter, trying to hold the thought of Jill—pretty Jill, who never did any harm to anyone—in my mind. She should not have died. None of them should have died.

"You...want...to escape...a fire?" he wheezed. "Fine...then. I hope you...freeze." His magic rose again, this time not to transform, but to open the door onto the Shadow Roads. He tumbled through it, me still on his back, arm still tight around his neck.

Some small time later, the shadows opened, and I stepped out alone. The Court looked at me for a long, appraising moment. In the back of the room, one of Father's doxies began to cry, covering her eyes with her hands. I watched them impassively.

Then Colleen stepped forward, head held high, and said, "The King is dead."

"The Prince has died in slaying him," I replied.

She nodded, accepting my ritual response. "Who claims the crown?"

I thought of Jill in the rafters of the Duke's Theatre, pulling me away before the play could end. I thought of Mercutio, who played the fool, and died for his sins.

Princes die when they become Kings. It is the way of things. But oh, I would miss the foolish Prince that I had been.

"Tybalt, King of the Court of Fogbound Cats," I said.

The Court roared its approval.

⚘

It was no small task to convince the Court of Cats to leave. Over and over, I repeated the Roane's message, until I began to understand, at least a little, why Father had been as he was. Cait Sidhe do not respond well to anything but shows of force. So I showed them force, drove them from Londinium with tooth and claw and threats of worse to come if they did not leave me be.

By the end of the first month, the knowes of the Divided Courts were empty shells, drained of everything that once made them so grand. I prowled their halls, watching the shadows creep in and claim them, and wondered how many of them would fall down into the dark, making the Court of the Cats even greater.

By the middle of the second month, only two Cait Sidhe remained in all of Londinium. "Come with me," said Colleen, grabbing my hand. "Please. I do not wish to see you burn."

"And I do not wish to see another sister gone to the night-haunts," I replied, pulling my hand away. "You are all the family I have left, Colleen, and I will have no other. You must go. When this city burns, I would know that you were far from here, free and happy and alive."

"What am I to do?"

I smiled a bit, caressing her cheek. "Find a theatre. Be their cat. Keep the rats from the costumes, and the shadows from the stage."

She nodded. "I wish you would come."

"And I wish you would go."

"Please."

"If I go, who will hold this Kingdom?" I looked at her solemnly. "Another King will come and establish a Court if I am not here to stop him. It is the nature of cats. And when the city burns, all their deaths will be on my conscience."

Colleen laughed. "A cat with a conscience. Is there anything more pitiful?"

"A king without a court, perhaps."

"Perhaps." She sighed. "Open roads, dear brother."

"Sweet shadows, and may the world forever run a step behind you."

"I will miss you," she said. Darting forward, she kissed my cheek. Then she whirled, pulling the shadows aside like the curtains of a stage. She dove into the darkness and was gone, leaving only me, and my ghosts, behind her.

☙❧

Day by day, I stalked the streets of London, waiting for the flames. And still, when they came, I was not prepared. A mortal bakery caught fire in the night, setting streets and blocks ablaze before anyone realized what was happening. The knowes of the Divided Courts, abandoned by their holders, were not fully sealed; pixies, fleeing for their lives, pried open a door they should have left alone. Their burning wings and hair ignited tapestries and carpets, and Londinium burned alongside her mortal sister.

Prophecies are tricky things. Had the custodians of those knowes not fled, would the doors have held their seals? Would the pixies have been left outside to burn, while all the Divided Courts and Court of Cats remained safely in our bolt holes?

I think not. I think that, once the fire was seen, it had to come, and the only question was who would be left to burn. But perhaps I think that because to do otherwise is to yield to madness. London is burning. Jill is dead, and with her, the boy who loved her as a sister and a friend. The night-haunts could not come for that simple Prince. He died in darkness all the same. I had become a King of Cats, and buried the Prince in shadows.

I sat on the edge of the Tower Bridge, watching London burn, and wondered whether the cold would ever leave me—or whether, in the measure of things, I would want it to. London is burning, Jill is dead. I am Tybalt, King of Cats, and all the rest...

All the rest is silence.

For Alligator.